To Caden

Love Gran

Grandpa -

This book belongs to

....

CLASSIC TREASURY
FAIRY STORIES

Compiled by Tig Thomas

Miles Kelly

First published in 2013 by Miles Kelly Publishing Ltd
Harding's Barn, Bardfield End Green, Thaxted, Essex, CM6 3PX, UK

Some of this material was first published in 2009 by
Miles Kelly Publishing Ltd as part of *50 Fairy Stories*

2 4 6 8 10 9 7 5 3 1

Publishing Director *Belinda Gallagher*
Creative Director *Jo Cowan*
Editorial Director *Rosie McGuire*
Senior Editor *Claire Philip*
Designers *Jo Cowan, Joe Jones, Michelle Foster, Venita Kidwai*
Production Manager *Elizabeth Collins*
Reprographics *Stephan Davis, Jennifer Hunt, Thom Allaway*

ISBN 978-1-78209-150-9

Printed in China

British Library Cataloguing-in-Publication Data
A catalogue record for this book is available from the British Library

ACKNOWLEDGEMENTS

The publishers would like to thank the following artists
who have contributed to this book:

Cover
Central image: Holly Clifton-Brown
Other elements: Alice Brisland at The Bright Agency, LenLis/Shutterstock.com,
kusuriuri/Shutterstock.com, Lana L/Shutterstock.com, Markovka/Shutterstock.com

Inside pages
Beehive Illustration: Elena Selivanova
The Bright Agency: Zdenko Basic, Mélanie Florian,
Jasmine Foster, Patricia Moffett, Katy Wright
Plum Pudding Illustration Agency: Christine Pym

Made with paper from a sustainable forest

www.mileskelly.net
info@mileskelly.net

CONTENTS

ENCHANTMENTS

CHILDREN AND FAIRIES

FAIRY HELPERS

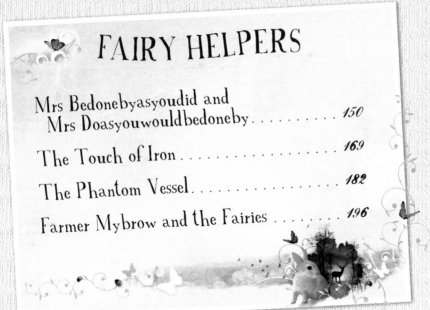

MAGIC AND MISCHIEF

VISITORS TO FAIRYLAND

I WISH, I WISH

ABOUT THE AUTHORS

Learn more about some of the famous
authors behind these much-loved stories.

Louisa M Alcott
1832–1888

The second of four daughters, Louisa May
Alcott's most famous book, *Little Women*
(1868), was based on her own experiences. It
describes a few months in the lives of the four
March sisters while their father is away from
home as Army Chaplain in the U.S. Civil War.

Eva's Visit to Fairyland

William Elliot Griffis
1843–1928

Both a minister and an author, American
William Elliot Griffis spent several years
teaching in Japan. He wrote over fifty books,
including many collections of fairy stories.

The Touch of Iron • A Boy that Visited Fairyland

J M Barrie
1860–1937

James Matthew Barrie grew up in Scotland. After graduating from the University of Edinburgh in 1882 he worked as a journalist, and three years later moved to London where he became a novelist and playwright. He is best known as the creator of Peter Pan, the boy who refused to grow up. The first stories about Peter were published in *The Little White Bird* (1902).

Peter's Two Wishes

Joseph Jacobs
1854–1916

Born in Australia, Jacobs studied in England and Germany as a young man, researching Jewish history. Eventually he settled in America, and, inspired by the Brothers Grimm, went on to edit five collections of fairy tales.

Connla and the Fairy Maiden • Fairy Ointment

About the Authors

E Nesbit
1858–1924

Edith Nesbit used the initial 'E' rather than 'Edith' to disguise the fact that she was a woman. She wrote more than forty books for children, and created the idea of mixing real-life characters and settings with magical elements. Her best-known books include *The Railway Children*, *Five Children and It* and *The Treasure Seekers*.

A Midsummer Night's Dream • Melisande • Beautiful as the Day

Katharine Pyle
1863–1938

Born into a warm and creative Quaker household, Katharine Pyle worked all her life as a writer and illustrator, like her brother, Howard Pyle (1853–1911). She worked on over fifty books, mostly for children, and these include fairy tales and animal stories.

The Counterpane Fairy

About the Authors

Sophia Morrison
1859–1917

Born on the Isle of Man, Morrison worked to promote the region's literature and music. She was a renowned authority on Manx folklore and fairylore, and wrote, collected and edited stories to preserve the island's language and history.

Billy Beg, Tom Beg, and the Fairies

Kate Douglas Wiggin
1856–1923

Born in Philadelphia, USA, Kate started the first free kindergarten in San Francisco. With her sister, Nora Archibald Smith (1859–1934), she set up a training school for kindergarten teachers, raising money for the school by writing stories.

The Smith and the Fairies • Drak, the Fairy

ABOUT THE ARTISTS

Holly Clifton-Brown A freelance illustrator living in London, Holly's work combines traditional painting with contemporary techniques to create a unique and imaginative visual language. Her work has been published in books and magazines worldwide.
Cover

Zdenko Basic Award-winning Croatian artist Zdenko uses a mixture of photography and illustration in his pieces, and also works in costume and set design, puppetry and animation.
The Smith and the Fairies • The Laird and the Man of Peace
A Boy That Visited Fairyland • The Counterpane Fairy
Billy Beg, Tom Beg, and the Fairies • Iktomi and the Muskrat

Mélanie Florian French illustrator Mélanie has always had a passion for drawing and telling stories. Her favourite medium is watercolour, for the freshness, lightness and freedom it offers. Her work has been published all over the world.
Connla and the Fairy Maiden • Christmas Every Day
The Phantom Vessel

Jasmine Foster As a child, Jasmine was drawn to illustrations with a dreamlike quality, and she now strives to capture that same sense in her own work.
A French Puck • Murdoch's Rath • The Prince with the Nose
Under the Sun • Sweet-one-darling and the Dream-fairies
Mrs Bedonebyasyoudid and Mrs Doasyouwouldbedoneby
The Fairy Wife • Rosanella

About the Artists

Christine Pym Since studying illustration for children's publishing in Wales, Christine has illustrated books, greetings cards and advent calendars, all in watercolour and pencil crayon.
_Melisande • Betty and the Wood Maiden • The Touch of Iron
The Fairy Fluffikins • Drak, the Fairy • Beautiful as the Day_

Patricia Moffett After 15 years as a designer and art buyer, Patricia decided to rekindle her desire to be an illustrator. Her favourite subjects are classics, mythology, fantasy and horror – anything that involves figures in an atmospheric setting.
_Eva's Visit to Fairyland • The Fairies and the Envious Neighbour
Peter's Two Wishes_

Elena Selivanova A graduate of Moscow State University of Printing Arts, Elena has been working as an illustrator with major publishing houses for more than 20 years.
Farmer Mybrow and the Fairies • The Fairy Cure

Katy Wright After growing up on a farm and studying illustration in Cornwall, UK, Katy packed up her belongings and moved to France. She can now be found sketching in her little studio in the heart of the beautiful city of Bordeaux.
A Midsummer Night's Dream

ENCHANTMENTS

A Midsummer Night's Dream

Retold by E Nesbit

*H*ermia and Lysander were lovers, but Hermia's father wished her to marry another man, named Demetrius.

Now, in Athens, where they lived, there was a wicked law, by which any girl who refused to marry according to her father's wishes, might be put to death. Hermia's father was so angry with her for refusing to do as he wished, that he actually brought her before the duke of Athens to ask that she might be killed, if she still refused to obey him. The duke gave her four days to think about it, and, at the end of that time, if she still refused to marry Demetrius, she would have to die.

Lysander of course was nearly mad with grief, and the best thing to do seemed to him for Hermia to run away to his aunt's house at a place beyond the reach of the law, and there he would come to her and marry her. But before she started out, Hermia told her friend, Helena, what she was going to do.

Helena had been Demetrius' sweetheart long before his marriage with Hermia had been thought of, and being very silly, like all jealous people, she could not see that it was not poor Hermia's fault that Demetrius wished to marry her instead of his own lady, Helena. She knew that if she told Demetrius that Hermia was going, as she was, to the wood outside Athens, he would follow her, 'and I can follow him, and at least I shall see him,' she said to herself. So she went to him, and betrayed her friend's secret.

Now this wood where Lysander was to meet Hermia, and where the other two had decided to follow them, was full of fairies, as most woods are, if one only had the eyes to see them, and in this wood on this night were the king and queen of the fairies, Oberon and Titania. Now fairies are very wise people, but now and then they can be quite as foolish as mortal folk. Oberon and Titania, who might have been as happy as the days were long, had thrown away all their joy in a foolish quarrel. They never met without saying disagreeable things to each other, and scolded each other so dreadfully that all their little fairy followers, for fear, would creep into acorn cups and hide there.

So, instead of keeping one happy court and dancing all night through in the moonlight as is the usual fairy manner, the king with his attendants wandered through one part of the wood, while the queen with hers kept state in another. And the cause of all this trouble was a little Indian boy whom Titania had taken to be one of her followers. Oberon wanted the child to follow him and be one of his fairy knights, but the queen would not give him up.

On this night, in a mossy moonlit glade, the king and queen of the fairies met.

"Ill met by moonlight, proud Titania," remarked the king.

"What! Jealous, Oberon?" answered the queen. "Why must you spoil everything with your quarrelling? Come, fairies, let us leave him. I am not friends with him now."

"It rests with you to make up the quarrel," said the king. "Give me that little Indian boy, and I will again be your humble servant and suitor."

"Please, set your mind at rest," said the queen, coldly. "Your whole fairy kingdom buys not that boy from me."

And she and her train rode off down the moonbeams.

"Well, go your ways," Oberon called after her, angrily. "But I will be even with you before you leave this wood."

Then Oberon called his favourite fairy, Puck. Puck was the spirit of mischief. He used to slip into the dairies and take the cream away, and get into the churn so that the butter would not come, and turn the beer sour, and lead people out of their way on dark nights and then laugh at them, and tumble people's stools from under them when they were going to sit down, and upset their hot ale over their chins when they were going to drink.

"Now," said Oberon to this little sprite, "fetch me the flower called Love-in-idleness. The juice of that little purple flower laid on the eyes of those who sleep will make them, when they wake, love the first thing they see. I will put some of the juice of that flower on my Titania's eyes, and when she wakes she will love the very first thing she sees, were it lion, bear, or wolf, or bull, or meddling monkey, or a busy ape."

While Puck was gone, Demetrius passed through the glade. He was followed by poor Helena, and still she told him how she loved him and reminded him of all his promises, and still he told her that he did not and could not love her, and that his promises were nothing. Oberon was sorry for poor Helena, and when Puck returned with the flower, he bade him follow Demetrius and put some of the juice on his eyes, so that he might love Helena when he woke and looked on her, as much as she loved him.

So Puck set off, and wandering through the wood found, not Demetrius, but Lysander and Hermia, sleeping peacefully. And so it was on Lysander's eyes that Puck put the juice. Unfortunately, when Lysander woke, he saw not his own Hermia, but Helena, who was walking through the wood looking for the cruel Demetrius. Directly he saw her, he loved her, and left his own lady, under the spell of the purple flower.

When Hermia woke she found Lysander gone, and wandered about the wood trying to find him. Puck went back and told Oberon what he had done, and Oberon soon found out the mistake, and set about looking for Demetrius. Having found him, he put some of the juice on his eyes. The first thing Demetrius saw when he woke was also Helena. So now Demetrius and Lysander were both following her through the wood,

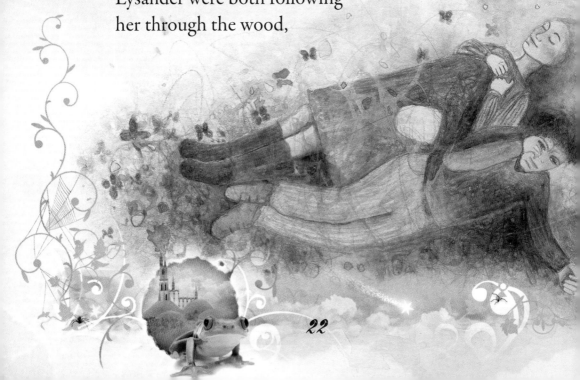

A Midsummer Night's Dream

and it was Hermia's turn to follow her lover as Helena had done before. The end of it was that Hermia and Helena began to quarrel, and Demetrius and Lysander went off to fight. Oberon was very sorry to see his kind scheme turn out so badly. So he said to Puck, "These two young men are going to fight. You must overhang the night with drooping fog, and lead them so astray, so that one will never find the other. When they are tired, they will fall asleep. Then drop this other herb on Lysander's eyes. It will give him his old sight and his old love. Then each man will have the lady who loves him, and they will all think that this has been only a midsummer night's dream."

So Puck did as he was told, and when the two had fallen asleep without meeting each other, Puck poured the juice on Lysander's eyes, and said:

"When thou wakest,
Thou takest
True delight
In the sight
Of thy former lady's eye:
Jack shall have Jill;
Nought shall go ill."

Meanwhile Oberon found Titania asleep on a bank where grew wild thyme, oxlips, and violets, and woodbine, musk-roses and eglantine. There Titania always slept a part of the night, wrapped in the enameled skin of a snake. Oberon stooped over her and laid the juice on her eyes, saying:

"What thou seest when thou wake,
Do it for thy true love take."

Now, it happened that when Titania woke the first thing she saw was a stupid clown, one of a party of players who had come out into the wood to rehearse their play. This clown had met with Puck, who had clapped an ass's head on his shoulders so that it looked as if it grew there. When Titania woke and saw this monster, she said, "What angel is this? Are you as wise as you are beautiful?"

"If I am wise enough to find my way out of this wood, that's enough for me," said the foolish clown.

"Do not desire to go out of the wood," said Titania. The spell of the love-juice was on her, and to her the clown seemed the most beautiful creature on the earth. "I love you," she went on. "Come with me, and I will give you fairies to attend on you."

So she called four fairies, whose names were Peaseblossom, Cobweb, Moth, and Mustardseed.

"You must attend this gentleman," said the queen. "Feed him with apricots and dewberries, purple grapes, green figs, and mulberries. Steal honey-bags for him from the bumble-bees, and with the wings of painted butterflies fan the moonbeams from his sleeping eyes."

"I will," said one of the fairies, and all the others said, "I will."

"Now, sit down with me," said the queen to the clown, "and let me stroke your dear cheeks, and stick musk-roses in your smooth, sleek head, and kiss your fair large ears, my gentle joy."

"Where's Peaseblossom?" asked the clown with

the ass's head. He did not care much about the
queen's affection, but he was very proud of having
fairies to wait on him.

"Ready," said Peaseblossom.

"Scratch my head, Peaseblossom," said the clown.
"Where's Cobweb?"

"Ready," said Cobweb.

"Kill me," said the clown, "the red bumble-bee on
the top of the thistle yonder, and bring me the
honey-bag. Where's Mustardseed?"

"Ready," said Mustardseed.

"Oh, I want nothing," said the clown. "Only just
help Cobweb to scratch. I must go to the barber's,
for methinks I am marvellous hairy about the face."

"Would you like anything to eat?" asked the fairy
queen, kindly.

"I should like some good dry oats," said the
clown – for his donkey's head made him desire
donkey's food – "and some hay to follow."

"Shall some of my fairies fetch you new nuts

from the squirrel's house?" asked the queen.

"I'd rather have a handful or two of good dried peas," said the clown. "But please don't let any of your people disturb me – I am going to sleep."

Then said the beautiful queen, "And I will wind thee in my arms."

And so when Oberon came along he found his queen lavishing kisses and endearments on a clown with a donkey's head.

And before he released her from the enchantment, he persuaded her to give him the little Indian boy he so much desired to have. Then he took pity on her, and threw some juice of the disenchanting flower on her pretty eyes, and then in a moment she saw plainly the donkey-headed clown she had been loving, and knew how foolish she had been.

Oberon took off the ass's head from the clown, and left him to finish his sleep with his own silly head lying on the thyme and violets.

Thus all was made plain and straight again.

ENCHANTMENTS

Oberon and Titania loved each other more than ever. Demetrius thought of no one but Helena, and Helena had never had any thought of anyone but Demetrius.

As for Hermia and Lysander, they were as loving a couple as you could meet in a day's march, even through a fairy wood.

So the four mortal lovers went back to Athens and were married, and the fairy king and queen live happily together in that very wood at this very day.

Melisande

By E Nesbit

When the Princess Melisande was born, her mother, the queen, wished to have a christening party, but the king put his foot down and said he would not have it.

"I've seen too much trouble come of christening parties," said he. "However carefully you keep your visiting-book, some fairy is sure to get left out, and you know what that leads to. We'll have no nonsense about it. We won't ask a single fairy, then none of them can be offended."

ENCHANTMENTS

"Unless they all are," said the queen.

And that was exactly what happened. When the king and the queen and the baby got back from the christening the great throne room was crammed with fairies of all ages and of all degrees of beauty and ugliness – good fairies and bad fairies, flower fairies and moon fairies, fairies like spiders and fairies like butterflies – and as the queen opened the door they all cried, with one voice, "Why didn't you ask me to your christening party?"

"I'm very sorry," said the poor queen, but Malevola pushed forward and said, "Hold your tongue," most rudely.

Malevola is the oldest, as well as the most wicked, of the fairies. "Don't begin to make excuses," she said, shaking her finger at the queen. "You know well enough what happens if a fairy is left out of a christening party. We are all going to give our christening presents now. I shall begin. The princess shall be bald."

Melisande

The queen nearly fainted as Malevola drew back.
But the king stepped forward too.

"Oh no you don't!" said he, raising his voice.
"How can you all be so very unfairylike? Have none
of you ever been to school? Have none of you

studied the traditions of your own race?"

"How dare you?" cried a fairy in a bonnet. "It is my turn, and I say the princess shall be—"

The king actually put his hand over her mouth.

"Look here," he said, "I won't have it. A fairy who breaks the rules of fairy history goes out – you know she does – like the flame of a candle. And all tradition shows that only one bad fairy is ever forgotten at a christening party and the good ones are always invited. So either this is not a christening party, or else you were all invited except one, and, by her own showing, that was Malevola. Try it, if you don't believe me. Give your nasty gifts to my innocent child – but as sure as you do, out you go, like a candle flame. Now, then, will you risk it?"

No one answered, but one by one all the fairies said goodbye and thanked the queen for the delightful afternoon they had spent with her.

When the very last fairy was gone the queen ran to look at the baby. She tore off its lace cap and burst into tears. For all the baby's downy golden hair came off with the cap, and the Princess Melisande was as bald as an egg.

"Don't cry, my love," said the king. "I have a wish lying by, which my fairy godmother gave me for a wedding present, but since then I've had nothing to wish for!"

"Thank you, dear," said the queen, smiling through her tears.

"I'll keep the wish till the baby grows up," the king went on. "And then I'll give it to her and if she likes to wish for hair, she can."

"Oh, won't you wish for it now?" said the queen.

"No, dearest. She may want something else more when she grows up. And besides, her hair may grow by itself."

But it never did. Princess Melisande grew up as beautiful as the sun and as good as gold, but never a hair grew on that little head of hers. The queen sewed her little caps of green silk, and the princess's pink and white face looked out of these like a flower peeping out of its bud. And every day as she grew older she grew dearer, and as she grew dearer she grew better, and as she grew more good she grew more beautiful.

Now, when she was grown up the queen said to the king, "My love, our dear daughter is old enough to know now what she wants. I think it is time you let her have the wish."

So the king unlocked his gold safe with the seven diamond-handled keys that hung at his girdle, and took out the wish and gave it to his daughter.

Then the queen said, "Dearest, for my sake, wish what I tell you."

"Why, of course I will," said Melisande. The queen whispered in her ear, and Melisande nodded. Then she said, aloud, "I wish I had golden hair that was a yard long, and that it would grow an inch every day, and grow twice as fast every time it was cut, and—"

"Stop!" cried the king. But the wish went off, and the next moment the princess stood smiling at him through a shower of golden hair.

"Oh, how lovely," said the queen. "What a pity you interrupted her, dear. What's the matter?"

"You'll know soon enough," said the king. "Come, let's be happy while we may. Give me a kiss, little Melisande, and then go to nurse and ask her to teach you how to comb your hair."

"I know how," said Melisande, "I've often combed mother's."

"Your mother has beautiful hair," said the king, "but I fancy you will find your own a little less easy to manage."

And, indeed, it proved to be just as the king said. The princess's hair began by being a yard long, and it grew another inch every night. If you know anything at all about the simplest sums you will see that in about five weeks her hair was about two yards long. This is a very inconvenient length. It

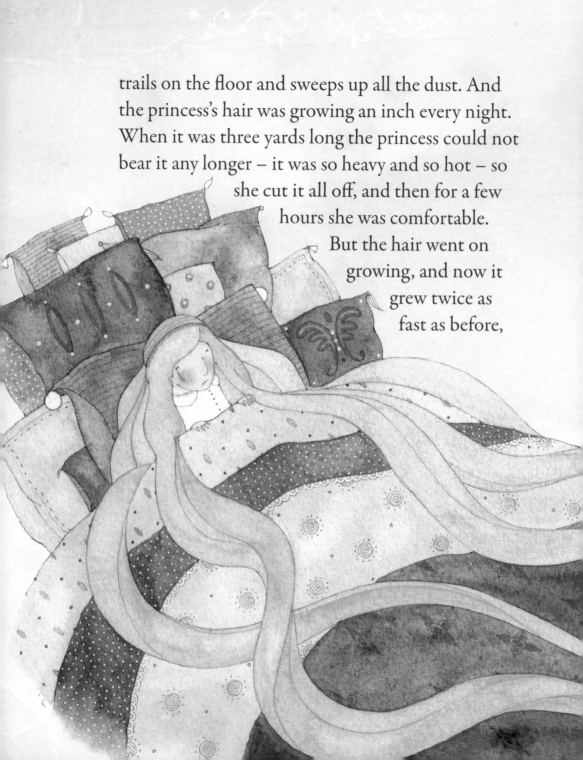

trails on the floor and sweeps up all the dust. And the princess's hair was growing an inch every night. When it was three yards long the princess could not bear it any longer – it was so heavy and so hot – so she cut it all off, and then for a few hours she was comfortable. But the hair went on growing, and now it grew twice as fast as before, so that in thirty-six days it was as long as ever. The poor princess cried with tiredness.

When she couldn't bear it anymore she cut her hair and was comfortable for a very little time. For the hair now grew four times as fast as at first, and in eighteen days it was as long as before, and she had to have it cut and so on, growing twice as fast after each cutting, till the princess would go to bed at night with her hair clipped short, and wake up in the morning with yards and yards and yards of golden hair flowing all about the room, so that she could not move without pulling her own hair, and nurse had to come and cut the hair off before she could get out of bed.

"I wish I was bald again," sighed poor Melisande. And still the hair grew and grew. Then the king said, "I shall write to my fairy godmother and see if something cannot be done."

ENCHANTMENTS

So he wrote and sent the letter by a skylark, and by return of bird came this answer:

> Why not advertise
> for a prince?
> Offer the usual reward.

So the king sent out his heralds all over the world to proclaim that any respectable prince with proper references should marry the Princess Melisande if he could stop her hair growing.

Then from far and near came trains of princes anxious to try their luck, and they brought all sorts of nasty things with them in bottles and round wooden boxes. The princess tried all the remedies, but she did not like any of them, and she did not like any of the princes, so in her heart she was rather glad that none of them made the least difference to her hair.

Melisande

The princess had to sleep in the throne room now, for no other room was big enough to hold her and her hair. When she woke in the morning the long high room would be quite full of her golden hair, packed tight and thick like wool in a barn. And every evening when her hair had been cut close to her head again, she would sit in her green silk gown at the window of the tallest tower and cry, and kiss the green caps she used to wear, and wish herself bald again. It was as she sat crying there on Midsummer Eve that she first saw Prince Florizel.

He was walking in the garden in the moonlight, and he looked up and she looked down, and for the first time Melisande, looking on a prince, wished that he might have the power to stop her hair from growing. As for the prince, he wished many things, and the first was granted him. For he said, "You are Melisande?"

"And you are Florizel?"

"There are many roses round your window," said

he to her, "and none down here."

She threw him one of three white roses she held in her hand.

Then he said, "If I can do what your father asks, will you marry me?"

"My father has promised that I shall," said Melisande, playing with the white roses in her hand.

"Dear princess," said Prince Florizel, "your father's promise is nothing to me. I want yours. Will you give it to me?"

"Yes," said she, and gave him the second rose.

"I want your hand."

"Yes," she said.

"And your heart with it."

"Yes," said the princess, and she threw down the third rose.

"Then," said he, "stay by your window and I will stay down here in the garden and watch. And when your hair has grown to the filling of your room, call to me and then do as I tell you."

"I will," said the princess. So at dewy sunrise the prince, lying on the turf beside the sundial, heard her voice. "Florizel! Florizel! My hair has grown so long that it is pushing me out of the window."

"Get out on to the windowsill," said he, "and twist your hair three times round the great iron hook that is there."

And she did.

43

ENCHANTMENTS

Then the prince climbed up the rose bush with his naked sword in his teeth, and he took the princess's hair in his hand about a yard from her head and said, "Jump!"

The princess jumped, and screamed, for there she was hanging from the hook by a yard and a half of her bright hair. The prince tightened his grasp of the hair and drew his sword across it.

Then he let her down gently by her hair till her feet were on the grass, and jumped down after her.

They stayed talking in the garden till all the shadows had crept under their proper trees and the sundial said it was breakfast time.

Then they went in to breakfast, and all the court crowded round to wonder and admire. For the princess's hair had not grown.

"How did you do it?" asked the king, shaking Florizel warmly by the hand.

"The simplest thing in the world," said Florizel, modestly. "You have always cut the hair off the princess. I just cut the princess off the hair."

"You are a young man of sound judgment," said the king, embracing him.

The princess kissed her prince a hundred times, and the very next day they were married. Everyone remarked on the beauty of the bride, and it was noticed that her hair was quite short – only five feet five and a quarter inches long – just down to her pretty ankles.

Connla and the Fairy Maiden

By Joseph Jacobs

onnla of the Fiery Hair was son of Conn of the Hundred Fights. One day as he stood by the side of his father on the height of Usna, he saw a maiden clad in strange attire coming towards him.

"Whence comest thou, maiden?" said Connla.

"I come from the Plains of the Ever Living," she said, "there where there is neither death nor sin. There we keep holiday always, nor need we help from any in our joy. And in all our pleasure we have no strife. And because we have our homes in the round green hills, men call us the Hill Folk."

The king and all with him wondered much to hear a voice when they saw no one. For save Connla alone, none saw the Fairy Maiden.

"To whom art thou talking, my son?" said Conn the king.

Then the maiden answered, "Connla speaks to a fair maid, whom neither death nor old age awaits. I love Connla, and now I call him away to the Plain of Pleasure, Moy Mell, where Boadag is king, nor has there been complaint or sorrow in that land since he has held the kingship. Oh, come with me, Connla of the Fiery Hair. A fairy crown awaits thee to grace thy comely face and royal form. Come, and never shall thy comeliness fade, nor thy youth, till the last awful day of judgment."

The king in fear at what the maiden said, which he heard though he could not see her, called aloud to his druid, Coran by name.

"Oh, Coran of the many spells," he said, "and of the cunning magic, I call upon thy aid. A task is upon me too great for all my skill and wit, greater than any laid upon me since I seized the kingship. A maiden unseen has met us, and by her power would take from me my dear, my comely son. If thou help not, he will be taken from thy king by woman's wiles and witchery."

Then Coran the druid stood forth and chanted his spells towards the spot where the maiden's voice had been heard. And none heard her voice again, nor could Connla see her longer. Only as she vanished before the druid's mighty spell, she threw an apple to Connla.

For a whole month from that day Connla would take nothing, either to eat or to drink, save only from that apple. But as he ate it grew again and always kept whole. And all the while there grew within him a mighty yearning and longing after

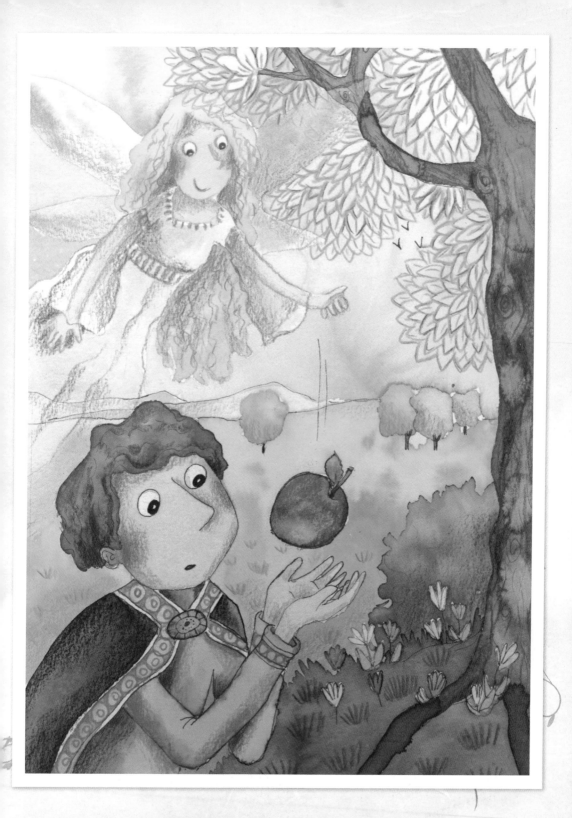

the maiden he had seen.

But when the last day of the month of waiting came, Connla stood once more by the side of his father on the Plain of Arcomin, and again he saw the maiden come towards him, and again she spoke to him.

"'Tis a glorious place that Connla holds among short-lived mortals awaiting the day of death. But now the folk of life beg and bid thee come with me to Moy Mell, the Plain of Pleasure, for they have learnt to know thee, seeing thee in thy home among thy dear ones."

When the king heard the maiden's voice he called out to his men, "Summon swift my druid, for I see the maiden has once more this day the power of speech."

Then the maiden addressed the king. "Oh, mighty Conn, fighter of a hundred fights, Coran the druid's power is little loved. It has no honour in the mighty land, peopled with so many of the upright. When the Law will come, it will do away with the druid's many magic spells that come from the lips of the false black demon."

Then the king observed that since the fairy maiden came Connla his son spoke to none that spoke to him. So Conn of the hundred fights said to him, "Is it to thy mind what the unseen woman says, my son?"

"'Tis hard upon me," said Connla. "I love my own folk above all things, but yet a longing seizes me for the maiden."

When the maiden heard Connla's reply, she said to him, "The ocean is not so strong as the waves of thy longing. Come with me in my curragh – the gleaming, crystal canoe. Soon we can reach Boadag's realm. I see the bright sun has started to sink, yet far as it is, we can reach it before dark. There is, too, another land worthy of thy journey, a land joyous to all that seek it. Only wives and maidens dwell there. If thou wilt, we can seek it and live there together in joy."

When the maiden ceased to speak, Connla of the Fiery Hair sprang into the the gleaming crystal canoe. And then they all, king and court, saw it glide away over the bright sea towards the setting sun. Away and away, till eye could see it no longer, and Connla and the fairy maiden went their way on the sea, and were no more seen.

Rosanella

By Comte de Caylus

*Inconstant, fickle, faithless – these are all words to describe
someone who cannot stay true to one love, but is always finding
a new person to fall in love with. But what happens when an
incurably fickle prince meets a princess no one can resist?*

Everybody knows that though the fairies live
hundreds of years they do sometimes die, and
especially as they pass one day in every week under
the form of some animal, when of course they are
liable to accident. It was in this way that death once
overtook the queen of the fairies, and it became

necessary to elect a new sovereign. After much discussion, it appeared that the choice lay between two fairies, one called Surcantine and the other Paridamie, and their claims were so equal that it was impossible to choose one over the other.

In the end, the fairy court decided that whichever of the two could show to the world the greatest wonder should be queen, but it was to be a special kind of wonder, no moving of mountains or any such common fairy tricks would do. Surcantine, therefore, decided that she would bring up a prince whom nothing could make faithful and constant to one love. While Paridamie decided to display to admiring mortals a princess so charming that no one could see her without falling in love with her. They were allowed to take their own time, and meanwhile the four oldest fairies were to attend to the affairs of the kingdom.

Now Paridamie had for a long time been very friendly with King Bardondon, who was a most

noble monarch, and whose court was the model of
what a court should be. His queen, Balanice, was
also charming – indeed it is rare to find a husband
and wife so perfectly of one mind
about everything.

They had one little
daughter, whom they had
named 'Rosanella', because
she had a pink rose
birthmark upon her throat.

On the night following the
assembly of fairies, Queen Balanice woke up with a
shriek, and when her maids of honour ran to see
what was the matter, they found she had had a
frightful dream.

"I thought," said she, "that my little daughter had
changed into a bouquet of roses, and that as I held it
in my hand a bird swooped down suddenly and
snatched it from me and carried it away."

The queen would not be comforted, and sent her

maids to see that all was well with the princess. So they ran, but they found the cradle empty. Though they sought high and low, not a trace of Rosanella could they find. The queen was beside herself with grief, and so, indeed, was the king, only being a man he did not say quite so much about his feelings.

He presently suggested to Balanice that they should spend a few days at one of their palaces in the country, and she agreed, since in her sorrow she no longer enjoyed the pleasures of town. One summer evening, as they sat together on a shady lawn shaped like a star, from which radiated twelve splendid avenues of trees, the queen looked round and saw a charming peasant girl approaching by each path, and that each girl carried something in a basket with the greatest care. As each girl drew near she laid her basket at Balanice's feet, saying, "Charming queen, may this be some slight comfort to you in your unhappiness!"

The queen hastily opened the baskets, and found

in each a lovely baby girl, about the same age as the little princess for whom she sorrowed so deeply. At first the sight of them renewed her grief, but presently their charms so gained upon her that she forgot her sadness in looking after the babies, providing them with maids, cradle-rockers, and ladies-in-waiting, and in sending hither and thither for swings and dolls and tops.

Oddly enough, every baby had upon its throat a tiny pink rose. The queen found it so difficult to decide on suitable names for all of them, that until she could settle the matter she chose a special colour for each girl, pink for one, purple for another, so that when they were all together they looked like nothing so much as a nosegay of flowers. As they grew older it became clear that though they were all remarkably intelligent, they differed one from another in character, so much so that they gradually ceased to be known as 'Ruby,' or 'Primrose,' or whatever might have been their colour, and the queen instead would say, "Where is my Sweet?" or "my Kind," or "my Happy."

Of course, with all these charms they had lovers by the dozen. Not only in their own court, but princes from afar, who were constantly arriving, attracted by the reports which were spread abroad. But these lovely girls, the first maids of honour, were as sensible as they were beautiful, and favoured no one.

But let us return to Surcantine. She had fixed upon the son of a king who was cousin to Bardondon, to bring up as her fickle prince. She had before, at his christening, given him all the graces of mind and body that a prince could possibly require, but now she redoubled her efforts, and spared no pains in adding every imaginable charm and fascination. So that whether he happened to be cross or amiable, splendidly or simply attired, serious or frivolous, he was always perfectly irresistible! In truth, he was a charming young fellow, since the fairy had given him the best heart in the world as well as the best head, and had left nothing to be desired except faithfulness. For it cannot be denied that Prince Mirliflor was a desperate flirt, and as fickle as the wind.

By the time he arrived at his eighteenth birthday there was not a heart left for him to conquer in his father's kingdom – they were all his own, and he was tired of everyone! Things were in this state when he was invited to visit the court of his father's cousin, King Bardondon.

Imagine his feelings when he arrived and was presented at once to twelve of the loveliest creatures in the world, and they all liked him as much as he liked each one of them, so that things came to such a pass that he was never happy a single instant without them. For could he not whisper soft speeches to Sweet, and laugh with Joy, while he looked at Beauty? And in his more serious moments what could be pleasanter than to talk to

Thoughtful upon some shady lawn, while he held the hand of Loving in his own, and all the others lingered near?

For the first time in his life he really loved, though the object of his devotion was not one person, but twelve, to whom he was equally attached, and even Surcantine was deceived into thinking that this was indeed the height of inconstancy. But Paridamie said not a word.

One day the queen gave a large garden party, and just as the guests were all assembled, and Prince Mirliflor was as usual dividing his attentions between the twelve beauties, a humming of bees was heard. The Rose-maidens, fearing their stings, uttered little shrieks, and fled to a distance from the rest of the company. Immediately, to the horror of all who were looking on, the bees pursued them, and, growing suddenly to an enormous size, pounced each upon a maiden and carried her off into the air, and in an instant they were all lost to view. This amazing occurrence plunged the whole court into the deepest sadness, and Prince Mirliflor, after giving way to the most violent grief at first, fell gradually into a state of such deep dejection that it was feared if nothing could rouse him he would certainly die.

Surcantine came in all haste to see what she could do for her darling, but he rejected with scorn all the portraits of lovely princesses which she offered him for his collection. In short, it was evident that he was in a bad way, and the fairy was at her wits' end.

One day, as he wandered about absorbed in melancholy reflections, he heard sudden shouts and exclamations of amazement, and if he had taken the trouble to look up he could not have helped being as astonished as everyone else, for through the air a chariot of crystal was slowly approaching, which glittered in the sunshine.

Six lovely maidens with shining wings drew it by

ENCHANTMENTS

rose-coloured ribbons,
while others, equally beautiful, were holding long
garlands of roses crossed above it, so as to form a
canopy. In it sat the Fairy Paridamie, and by her side
a princess whose beauty dazzled all who saw her.

Rosanella

At the foot of the great
staircase they descended, and
proceeded to the queen's apartments, though
everyone had run together to see this marvel, till it
was difficult to make a way through the crowd, and
exclamations of wonder rose on all sides at the
loveliness of the strange princess. "Great queen,"
said Paridamie, "permit me to restore to you your
daughter Rosanella, whom I stole out of her cradle."

After the first transports of joy were over the
queen said to Paridamie, "But my twelve lovely
ones, are they lost to me for ever? Shall I never see
them again?"

But Paridamie only said, "Very soon you will
cease to miss them!" in a tone that evidently meant
'Don't ask me any more questions.' Then mounting

again into her chariot she swiftly disappeared.

The news of his beautiful cousin's arrival was soon carried to the prince, but he had hardly the heart to go and see her. However, it became absolutely necessary that he should pay his respects, and he had scarcely been five minutes in her presence before it seemed to him that she combined in her own charming person all the gifts and graces which had so attracted him in the twelve Rose-maidens whose loss he had so truly mourned.

And after all it is really more satisfactory to be in love with one person at a time. So it came to pass that before he knew where he was he was entreating his lovely cousin to marry him, and the moment the words had left his lips, Paridamie appeared, smiling and triumphant, in the chariot of the queen of the fairies, for by that time they had all heard of her success, and declared her to have earned the kingdom. She had to give a full account of how she had stolen Rosanella from her cradle, and divided

Rosanella

her character into twelve parts, that each might charm Prince Mirliflor, and when once more united might cure him of his inconstancy once and for all.

And as one more proof of the fascination of the whole Rosanella, I may tell you that even the defeated Surcantine sent her a wedding gift, and was present at the ceremony which took place as soon as the guests could arrive. Prince Mirliflor was faithful only to his adored Rosanella for the rest of his life. And indeed who would not have been in his place?

As for Rosanella, she loved him as much as all the twelve beauties put together, so they reigned in peace and happiness to the end of their long lives.

The Smith and the Fairies

By Kate Douglas Wiggin

It was a superstition in Celtic lands that fairies stole babies and left changelings (fairy babies) in their place. In this story the fairies are called by their Gaelic name of Daione Sith, *and the word for a changeling is* Sibhreach. *A* dirk *is a short knife.*

Years ago there lived in Crossbrig a smith of the name of MacEachern. This man had an only child, a boy of about thirteen or fourteen years of age, cheerful, strong and healthy. All of a sudden he fell ill, took to his bed and moped whole days away.

The Smith and the Fairies

No one could tell what was the matter with him, and the boy himself could not, or would not, tell how he felt. He was wasting away fast – getting thin, old, and yellow – and his father and all his friends were afraid that he would die.

After the boy had been lying in this condition for a long time, getting neither better nor worse (but with an extraordinary appetite) an old man, well known for his knowledge of out-of-the-way things, walked into the smith's workshop. The smith told him the occurrence which had clouded his life.

The old man looked grave as he listened, and after sitting a long time pondering over all he had heard, gave his opinion, "It is not your son you have got. The boy has been carried away by the Daione Sith, and they have left a Sibhreach in his place."

"Alas! And what then am I to do?" said the smith. "How am I ever to see my own son again?"

"I will tell you how," answered the old man. "But, first, to make sure that it is not your own son you have got, take as many empty eggshells as you can get, go into his room, spread them out carefully before his sight, then proceed to draw water with them, carrying them two and two in your hands as if they were a great weight, and arrange them when full, around the fire."

The smith proceeded to carry out all his instructions. He had not been long at work before there arose from the bed a loud shout of laughter, and the voice of the seemingly sick boy exclaimed, "I am eight hundred years of age, and I have never seen the like of that before." The smith returned and told the old man.

"Well, now," said the old man to him, "did I not tell you that it was not your son you had – your son is in Borracheill in a digh there (that is, a round green hill frequented by fairies). Get rid as soon as possible of this intruder, and I think I may promise you your son. You must light a very large and bright fire before the bed on which this stranger is lying.

The Smith and the Fairies

He will ask you, 'What is the use of such a fire as that?' Answer him at once, 'You will see that presently!' and then seize him, and throw him into the middle of it. If it is your own son you have got, he will call out to you to save him, but if not, the thing will fly through the roof."

The smith again followed the old man's advice. He kindled a large fire, answered the question put to him as he had been directed to do, and seizing the child flung him in without hesitation. The Sibhreach gave an awful yell, and sprang through the roof, where a hole had been left to let the smoke out.

The old man told the smith that on a certain night the green round hill, where the fairies kept the boy, would be open. On that date the smith, having provided himself with a Bible and a dirk, was to proceed to the hill. He would hear singing and dancing, and much merriment going on, but he was to advance boldly – the Bible he carried would be a safeguard to him against danger from the fairies.

On entering the hill he was to stick the dirk in the threshold, to prevent the hill from closing upon him. "And then," said the old man, "on entering you will see a spacious apartment before you, and there, standing far within, working at a forge, you will also see your son. When you are questioned, say you come to seek him, and will not go without him."

Not long after this, the time came round, and the smith sallied forth, prepared as instructed. Sure enough as he approached the hill, there was a light where light was seldom seen before. Soon after, a sound

The Smith and the Fairies

of piping, dancing, and joyous merriment reached the anxious father on the night wind.

Overcoming every impulse of fear, the smith approached the threshold steadily, stuck the dirk into it as directed, and entered. Protected by the Bible he carried on his breast, the fairies could not touch him, but they asked him, with a good deal of displeasure, what he wanted there. He answered, "I want my son, whom I see down there, and I will not go without him."

The fairies, incensed, seized the smith and his son, and throwing them out of the hill, flung the dirk after them, and in an instant all was dark.

For a year and a day the boy never did a turn of work, and hardly ever spoke a word. At last one day, sitting by his father and watching him finishing a sword, he suddenly exclaimed, "That is not the way to do it." And taking the tools from his father's hands he set to work himself in his place, and soon fashioned a sword, the like of which was never seen

71

ENCHANTMENTS

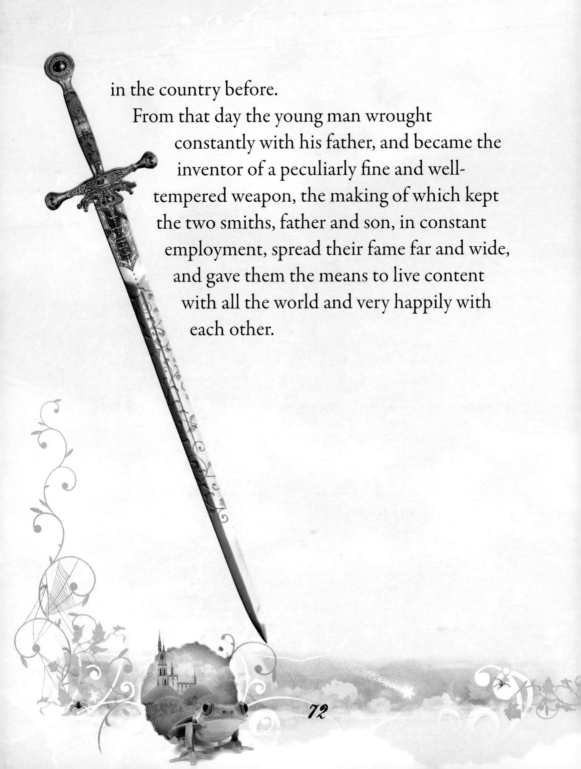

in the country before.

From that day the young man wrought
constantly with his father, and became the
inventor of a peculiarly fine and well-
tempered weapon, the making of which kept
the two smiths, father and son, in constant
employment, spread their fame far and wide,
and gave them the means to live content
with all the world and very happily with
each other.

The Prince with the Nose

By Dinah Maria Mulock Craik

*T*here was once a king who was passionately in love with a beautiful princess, but she could not marry because a magician had enchanted her. The king went to a good fairy to inquire what he should do. Said the fairy, after receiving him graciously, "Sir, I will tell you a secret. The princess will be obliged to marry any person nimble enough to walk upon her cat's tail."

'That will not be very difficult,' thought the king to himself, and departed, resolving to trample the cat's tail to pieces rather than not succeed in walking upon it. He went immediately to the palace of his fair mistress and the cat. The animal came in front of him, and the king lifted up his foot, thinking nothing would be so easy as to tread on the tail, but he found himself mistaken. Minon – that was the creature's name – twisted itself round so sharply that the king only hurt his own foot by stamping on the floor.

For eight days he pursued the cat everywhere – up and down the palace from morning till night. But with no success – the tail seemed made of quicksilver, so very lively was it. At last the king had the good fortune to catch Minon sleeping, and – *tramp, tramp* – he trod on the tail with all his force.

Minon woke up, and immediately changed from a cat into a large, fierce-looking man, who regarded the king with flashing eyes.

The Prince with the Nose

"You have broken the enchantment in which I held the princess, but I will be revenged. You shall have a son with a nose as long as this," – he made in the air a curve of half a foot – "yet he shall believe it is just like all other noses, and shall be always unfortunate till he has found out it is not. And if you ever tell anybody of this threat, you shall die on the spot." So saying, the magician disappeared.

The king, who was at first terrified, soon began to laugh at this adventure. 'My son might have a worse misfortune than too long a nose,' thought he. 'I will find the princess, and marry her at once.'

He did so, but he only lived a few months after, and died before his little son was born, so that nobody knew anything about the secret of the nose.

The little prince was so much wished for that when he came into the world they agreed to call him Prince Wish. He had beautiful blue eyes, and a sweet little mouth, but his nose was so big that it covered half his face. The queen's ladies tried to

satisfy her by telling her that the nose would grow
smaller as the prince grew bigger, and that if it did
not, a large nose was indispensable to a hero. The
queen listened eagerly to this comfort. She grew so
used to the prince's nose that it did not seem to her
any larger than ordinary noses of the court, where,
in process of time, everybody with a long nose was
very much admired, and the unfortunate people
who had only snubs were taken little notice of.

Great care was observed in the education of the
prince, and as soon as he could speak they told him
all sorts of amusing tales, in which all the bad
people had short noses, and all the good people had
long ones. His tutor taught him history, and
whenever any great king was referred to, the tutor
always took care to mention that he had a long
nose. The royal apartments were filled with pictures
and portraits having this peculiarity, and Prince
Wish began to regard the length of his nose as his
greatest perfection.

When he was twenty years old his mother and
his people wished him to marry. They procured for
him the portraits of many princesses, but the one he
preferred was Princess Darling, daughter of a
powerful monarch and heiress to several kingdoms.
Alas! With all her beauty, this princess had one
great misfortune, a little turned-up nose, which,
everyone else said, made her only the more
bewitching. But here, in the kingdom of
Prince Wish, the courtiers were thrown by it into
the utmost perplexity. They were in the habit of
laughing at all small noses, but how dared they
make fun of the nose of Princess Darling?

They would have found themselves in constant
difficulties, had not one clever person struck upon a
bright idea. He said that though it was necessary for
a man to have a long nose, women were very
different creatures, and that a learned man had
discovered in an old manuscript that the celebrated
Cleopatra, queen of Egypt and the beauty of the

ancient world, also had a turned-up nose. At this information Prince Wish was so delighted that he immediately sent off ambassadors to ask for Princess Darling's hand in marriage.

She accepted his offer at once, and returned with the ambassadors. He made all haste to meet and welcome her, but when she was only three leagues distant from his capital, before he had time even to kiss her hand, the magician who had once assumed the shape of his mother's cat, Minon, appeared in the air and carried her off before the prince's very eyes.

Prince Wish, almost beside himself with grief, declared that nothing should induce him to return to his throne and kingdom till he had found Princess Darling. He mounted a good horse, laid the reins on the animal's neck, and let him take him wherever he would.

The horse entered a wide, extended plain, and trotted on steadily the whole day without finding a single house. Master and beast began almost to faint with hunger, and Prince Wish might have wished himself safe at home again, had he not discovered, just as night was falling, a dark cavern. Outside the cavern was a bright little lantern, and sitting in its light was a tiny woman – she looked as though she could easily have been more than a hundred years old.

She put on her spectacles the better to look at the stranger, and he noticed that her nose was so small that the spectacles would hardly stay on. Then the prince and the fairy – for it was a fairy – burst into a mutual fit of laughter.

"What a funny nose!" cried the one.

"Not so funny as yours, madam," returned the other. "But pray let us leave our noses alone, and be good enough to give me something to eat, for I am dying with hunger, and so is my poor horse."

"With all my heart," answered the fairy. "Although your nose is ridiculously long, you are no less the son of one of my best friends. I loved your father like a brother. He had a very handsome nose."

"What is wanting to my nose?" asked Wish, rather savagely.

"Oh! Nothing at all. On the contrary, there is a great deal too much of it, but never mind, one may be a very honest man, and yet have too big a nose. I will give you some supper directly, and while you eat it I will tell you my history in six words, for I hate much talking. A long tongue is as unbearable as a long nose, and I remember when I was young how much I used to be admired because I was not a talker, indeed, my mother, for poor as you see me now, I am the daughter of a great king, who always—"

ENCHANTMENTS

'Hang the king your father!' Prince Wish was about to exclaim, but he stopped himself, and only observed that however the pleasure of her conversation might make him forget his hunger, it could not have the same effect upon his horse, who was really starving.

The fairy, pleased at his civility, called her servants and bade them supply him with all he needed. "And," added she, "I must say you are very polite and good-tempered, in spite of your nose."

'What has the old woman to do with my nose?' thought the prince. 'If I were not so very hungry I would soon show her what she is – a regular old gossip and chatterbox. She fancies she talks little, indeed! One must be very foolish not to know one's own defects. This comes of being born a fairy. Flatterers have spoiled her, and persuaded her that she talks little.'

While the prince thus meditated, the servants were laying the table, the fairy asking them a

The Prince with the Nose

hundred unnecessary questions, simply for the pleasure of hearing herself talk. 'Well,' thought Wish, 'I am delighted that I came hither, if only to learn how wise I have been in never listening to flatterers, who hide from us our faults, or make us believe they are perfections. But they could never deceive me. I know all my own weak points, I trust.' And truly he believed he did.

So he went on eating contentedly, nor stopped till the old fairy began to address him.

"Prince," said she, "will you be kind enough to turn a little? Your nose casts such a shadow that I cannot see what is on my plate. And, as I was saying, your father admired me and always made me welcome at court. What is the court etiquette there now? Do the ladies still go to assemblies, balls, promenades? I beg your pardon for laughing, but how very long your nose is."

"I wish you would cease to speak of my nose," said the prince, becoming annoyed. "It is what it is, and I do not desire it any shorter."

"Oh! I see that I have vexed you," returned the fairy. "Nevertheless, I am one of your best friends, and so I shall take the liberty of always—"

She would doubtless have gone on talking till midnight, but the prince, unable to bear it any longer, here interrupted her, thanked her for her hospitality, bade her a hasty adieu, and rode away.

He travelled for a long time, half over the world, but he heard no news of Princess Darling. However, in each place he went to, he heard one remarkable fact – the great length of his own nose. The little boys in the streets jeered at him, the peasants stared at him, and the more polite ladies and gentlemen whom he met in society used to try in vain to keep from laughing, and to get out of his way as soon as they could. So the poor prince became gradually quite forlorn and solitary. He thought all the world was mad, but still he never thought of there being anything queer about his own nose.

The Prince with the Nose

At last the old fairy, who, though she was a chatterbox, was very good-natured, saw that he was almost breaking his heart. She felt sorry for him, and wished to help, for she knew the enchantment which hid from him the Princess Darling could not be broken till he discovered his own defect. So she went in search of the princess, and being more powerful than the magician, she took her away from him, and shut her up in a palace of crystal, which she placed on the road which Prince Wish had to pass.

He was riding along, very melancholy, when he saw the palace, and at its entrance was a room made of glass, in which sat his beloved princess, smiling and beautiful as ever. He leaped from his horse, and ran towards her. She held out her hand for him to kiss, but he could not get at it for the glass. Transported with eagerness and delight, he dashed his sword through the crystal, and succeeded in breaking a small opening, to which she put up her beautiful rosy mouth. But it was in vain, Prince Wish could not approach it. He twisted his neck about, and turned his head on all sides, till at length, putting up his hand to his face, he discovered the impediment.

"It must be confessed," exclaimed he, "that my nose is too long."

That moment the glass walls all split asunder, and the old fairy appeared, leading Princess Darling.

"Admit, prince," said she, "that you are very much obliged to me, for now the enchantment is ended. You may marry the object of your choice. But," added she, smiling, "I fear I might have talked to you forever on the subject of your nose, and you would not have believed me in its remarkable length, until it became an obstacle to your own inclinations. Now behold it!" and she held up a crystal mirror. And will you be satisfied to be no different from other people?"

"Perfectly," said Prince Wish, who found his nose had shrunk to an ordinary length. And, taking the Princess Darling by the hand, he kissed her, courteously, affectionately and satisfactorily. Then they departed to their own country, and lived very happy all their days.

CHILDREN
AND FAIRIES

Sweet-one-darling and the Dream-fairies

By Eugene Field

A wonderful thing happened one night.
Sweet-one-darling was lying in her cradle,
and she was trying to make up her mind whether
she should go to sleep or keep awake. Sweet-one-
darling was ready for sleep. She had on her
nightgown and nightcap, and her mother had kissed
her goodnight. But the day had been so pleasant
that Sweet-one-darling was unwilling to give it up.

Sweet-one-darling and the Dream-fairies

A cricket was chirping, and some folk believe
that the cricket is in league with the Dream-fairies.
They say that what sounds to us like a faint chirping
is actually the call of the cricket to the Dream-fairies
to tell those creatures that it is time for them to
come with their dreams.

Then, all of a sudden, there was a sound as of the
rustle of silken wings, and the next moment two of
the sweetest fairies you ever saw were standing
upon the windowsill, just over the honeysuckle.

CHILDREN AND FAIRIES

They had come from Somewhere, and it was evident that they were searching for somebody, for they peered cautiously and eagerly into the room. One was dressed in a bright yellow suit of butterfly silk and the other wore a suit of dark-grey mothzine, which (as perhaps you know) is a dainty fabric made of the fine strands which grey moths spin. Both of these fairies together would not have weighed much more than the one-sixteenth part of four dewdrops.

"Sweet-one-darling! Oh, Sweet-one-darling!" they cried softly. "Where are you?"

Sweet-one-darling pretended that she did not hear, and she cuddled down close in her cradle and laughed, all to herself. The mischievous little thing knew well enough whom they were calling but she meant to fool them and hide from them awhile – that is why she did not answer. But nobody can hide from the Dream-fairies, and least of all could Sweet-one-darling hide from them, for presently her

laughter betrayed her and the two Dream-fairies
perched on her cradle – one at each side – and
looked smilingly down upon her.

"Hello!" said Sweet-one-darling.

This was the first time I had ever heard her speak,
and I did not know till then that even wee little
babies talk with fairies, particularly Dream-fairies.

"Hello, Sweet-one-darling!" said Gleam-of-the-
dark, for that was the name of the Dream-fairy in
the dark-grey mothzine.

"And hello from me, too!" cried Frisk-and-glitter,
the other visitor – the one in the butterfly-silk suit.

"You have come earlier than usual," suggested
Sweet-one-darling.

"No, indeed," answered Frisk-and-glitter, "But
the day has been so happy that it has passed quickly.
For that reason you should be glad to see me, for I
bring dreams of the day – the beautiful golden day,
with its sunlight, its grace of warmth, and its mirth
and play."

CHILDREN AND FAIRIES

"And I," said Gleam-of-the-dark, "I bring dreams, too. But my dreams are of the night, and they are full of the gentle, soothing music of the winds, of the whisper of pines, and of the chirps of crickets! You shall see the things of Fairyland and of Dreamland, and of all the mysterious countries that compose the vast world of Somewhere, away out beyond the silvery mist of night."

"Oh!" cried Sweet-one-darling. "I should never be able to make a choice between you two. I would love to have the play of the daytime brought back to me, and I am quite as sure that I want to see all the pretty sights that are unfolded by the dreams which Gleam-of-the-dark brings."

"You have no need to feel troubled," said Frisk-and-glitter, "for you are not expected to make any choice between us. We have our own way of solving the question, as you shall presently understand."

Then the Dream-fairies explained that whenever they came of an evening to bring their dreams to a

little child they climbed onto the child's eyelids and tried to rock them down. Gleam-of-the-dark would stand and rock upon one eyelid and Frisk-and-glitter would stand and rock upon the other.
If Gleam-of-the-dark's eyelid closed first, the child would dream the dreams Gleam-of-the-dark brought it. If Frisk-and-glitter's eyelid closed first, why, then, of course, the child dreamt the dreams Frisk-and-glitter brought.

"But suppose," suggested Sweet-one-darling, "suppose both eyelids close at the same instant? Which one of you fairies has his own way then?"

"Ah, in that event," said they, "neither of us wins, and, since neither wins, the sleeper does not dream at all, but awakes next morning from a sound, dreamless, refreshing sleep."

Sweet-one-darling was not sure that she fancied this alternative, but of course she could not help herself. So she let the two little Dream-fairies flutter across her shoulders and clamber up her cheeks to their proper places upon her eyelids. Gracious! How heavy they seemed when they stood on her eyelids! As I told you before, their actual combined weight hardly exceeded the sixteenth part of four dewdrops, yet when they are perched on a little child's eyelids (tired eyelids at that) it really seems sometimes as if they weighed a tonne! It was just all she could do to keep her eyelids open, yet Sweet-one-darling was determined to be strictly fair. She loved both the Dream-fairies equally well, and she would not for all the world have shown either one any favouritism.

Well, there the two Dream-fairies stood on Sweet-one-darling's eyelids, each one trying to rock his particular eyelid down, and each one sung his little lullaby in the pipingest voice imaginable. This was very soothing, as you would suppose. It was the most exciting contest (for an amicable one) I ever saw. As for Sweet-one-darling, she seemed to be lost presently in the magic of the Dream-fairies, and

although she has never said a word
about it to me I am quite sure
that, while her dear eyelids
drooped and drooped and
drooped to the rocking and
singing of the Dream-fairies,
she enjoyed a confusion of
all those precious things
promised by her two
fairy visitors.

Yes, I am sure that from
under her drooping eyelids she beheld
the scenes of the day mingled with peeps of
fairyland. And when at last she was fast asleep I
could not say for certain which of her eyelids had
closed first, so simultaneous was the downfall of her
long dark lashes upon her flushed cheeks. I meant
to have asked the Dream-fairies about it, but before
I could do so they whisked out of the window and
away with their dreams to a very sleepy little boy

who was waiting for them somewhere in the neighbourhood. So you see I am unable to tell you which of the Dream-fairies won. Maybe neither did, maybe Sweet-one-darling's sleep that night was dreamless. I have questioned her about it and she will not answer me.

This is all the wonderful tale I had to tell. Maybe it will not seem so wonderful to you, for perhaps you, too, have felt the Dream-fairies rocking your eyelids down with gentle lullaby music. Perhaps you, too, know all the precious dreams they bring. In that case you will bear witness that my tale, even though it be not wonderful, is strictly true.

Betty and the
Wood Maiden

By A H Wratislaw

*In this story, Betty spins rough flax into thread. She uses a spindle
(stick) to spin the thread, but she is too poor to own a distaff (the tool
which holds the raw fibre before it is spun). Her mother then reels
the thread off the spindle into skeins (coils) ready for weaving.*

*B*etty was a little girl. Her mother was a widow,
and had no more of her property left than a
dilapidated cottage and two she-goats, but Betty
was, nevertheless, always cheerful. From spring to
autumn she pastured the goats in the birch wood.

Whenever she went from home, her mother always gave her in a basket a slice of bread and a spindle, with the order, "Let it be full."

As she had no distaff, she used to twine the flax round her head. Betty took the basket and skipped off singing merrily after the goats to the birch wood. When she got there, the goats went after pasture, and Betty sat under a tree, drew the fibres from her head with her left hand, and let down the spindle with her right so that it just hummed over the ground, and then she would sing till the wood echoed. When the sun indicated midday, she put aside her spindle, called the goats, and after giving them each a morsel of bread that they mightn't stray from her, bounded into the wood for a few strawberries or any other woodland fruit that might happen to be just then in season, that she might have dessert to her bread.

When she had finished her meal, she sprang up, danced and sang. After her dance, she spun again industriously, and in the evening, when she drove the goats home, her mother never had to scold her for bringing back her spindle empty.

Once, when according to custom, exactly at midday, after her scanty dinner, she was getting ready for a dance, all of a sudden – where she came, there she came – a very beautiful maiden stood before her. She had on a white dress as fine as gossamer, golden-coloured hair flowed from her head to her waist, and on her head she wore a garland of woodland flowers. Betty was struck dumb with astonishment. The maiden smiled at her, and said in an attractive voice, "Betty, are you fond of dancing?"

When the maiden spoke so prettily to her, Betty's terror quitted her, and she answered, "Oh, I should like to dance all day long!"

"Come, then, let's dance together. I'll teach you!" So spoke the maiden, tucked her dress up on one side, took Betty by the waist, and began to dance with her. As they circled, such delightful music sounded over their heads, that Betty's heart skipped within her. It was a company of choice musicians that had come together at the beck of the beautiful maiden – nightingales, larks, linnets, goldfinches, greenfinches, thrushes, blackbirds, and a very skilful mockingbird.

Betty's cheek flamed, her eyes glittered, she forgot her task and her goats, and only gazed at her partner, who twirled before and round her with the most charming movements, and so lightly that the grass didn't even bend beneath her delicate foot. They danced from noon till eve, and Betty's feet were neither wearied nor painful. Then the beautiful maiden stopped, the music ceased, and as she came so she disappeared. Betty looked about her. The sun was setting behind the wood. She suddenly remembered the unspun flax, and saw that her spindle, which was lying on the grass, was by no means full. She called the goats, and drove them home. The goats, hearing no merry song behind them, looked round to see whether their own shepherdess was really following them. Her mother, too, wondered, and asked her daughter whether she was ill, as she didn't sing.

"No, mother dear, I'm not ill, but my throat is dry from singing, and therefore I don't sing," said Betty in excuse, and went to put away the spindle and the unspun flax.

Knowing that her mother was not in the habit of reeling up the yarn at once, she intended to make up the next day what she had neglected to do the first day, and therefore did not say a word to her mother about the beautiful maiden.

The next day Betty again drove the goats as usual

to the birch wood, and sang to herself again merrily. On arriving at the birch wood the goats began to pasture, and she sat under the tree and began to spin industriously, The sun indicated midday. Betty went off for strawberries, and after returning began to eat her dinner and chatter with the goats. "Ah, my little goats, I mustn't dance today," sighed she.

"And why mustn't you?" spoke a pleasing voice, and the beautiful maiden stood beside her, as if she had dropped from the clouds.

Betty answered modestly, "Excuse me, beautiful lady, I can't dance with you, because I should again fail to perform my task of spinning, and my mother would scold me. Today, before the sun sets, I must make up what I left undone yesterday."

"Only come and dance, and before the sun sets help will be found for you," said the maiden. She tucked up her dress, took Betty round the waist, the musicians sitting on the birch branches struck up, and the two dancers began to whirl.

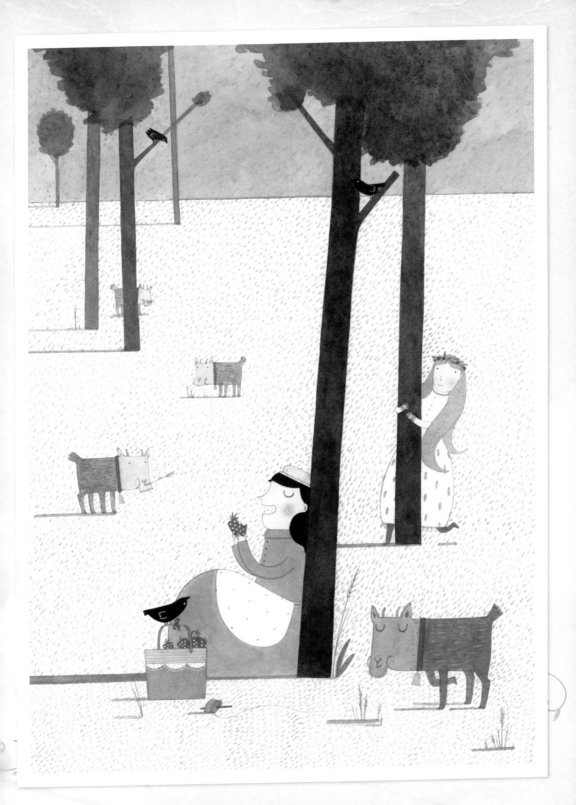

At last the dancers stopped, the music ceased, the sun was on the verge of setting. Betty clapped her hand on the top of her head, where the unspun flax was twined, and began to cry. The beautiful maiden put her hand on Betty's head, took off the flax, twined it round the stem of a slender birch, seized the spindle, and began to spin. The spindle grew fuller before her eyes, and before the sun set behind the wood all the yarn was spun, as well as that which Betty had not finished the day before.

While giving the full spool into the girl's hand the beautiful maiden said, "Reel, and grumble not – remember my words – Reel, and grumble not!" After these words she vanished, as if the ground had sunk in beneath her. Betty was content, and thought on her way home, 'If she is so good and kind as to fill the spindle, I will dance with her again if she comes again.' But her mother gave her no cheerful welcome. Wishing in the course of the day to reel the yarn, she saw that the spindle was not full, and was therefore out of humour.

"What were you doing yesterday that you didn't finish your task?" asked her mother reprovingly.

"Pardon, mother – I danced a little too long," said Betty humbly, and, showing her mother the spindle, added, "Today it is more than full to make up for it." Her mother said no more, but went to milk the goats, and Betty put the spindle away. She wished to tell her mother of her adventure, but bethought herself again, 'No, not unless she comes again, and then I will ask her what kind of person she is, and will tell my mother.'

The third morning, as usual, she drove the goats to the birch wood. The goats began to pasture. Betty sat under the tree, and began to sing and spin. The sun indicated midday. Betty laid her spindle on the grass, gave each of the goats a morsel of bread, collected strawberries, ate her dinner, and while giving the crumbs to the birds, said, "My little goats, I will dance to you today!" She jumped up, folded her hands, and was just going to see if she could manage to dance as prettily as the beautiful maiden, when all at once she herself stood before her.

"Let's go together, together!" said she to Betty, seized her round the waist, and at the same moment the music struck up over their heads, and the maidens circled round with flying step. Betty forgot her spindle and her goats, saw nothing but the beautiful maiden, whose body bent in every direction like a willow-wand, and thought of nothing but the delightful music, in tune with which her feet bounded of their own accord. They danced from midday till evening. Then the maiden stopped, and the music ceased.

Betty looked round. The sun was behind the wood. With tears she clasped her hands on the top of her head, and turning in search of the half-empty spindle, lamented about what her mother would say to her.

"Give me your basket," said the beautiful maiden.

Betty and the Wood Maiden

"I will make up to you for what you have left undone today."

Betty handed her the basket, and the maiden disappeared for a moment, and afterwards handed Betty the basket again, saying, "Not now – look at it at home," and was gone, as if the wind had blown her away.

Betty was afraid to peep into the basket immediately, but halfway home she couldn't restrain herself. The basket was as light as if there was just nothing in it. She couldn't help looking to see whether the maiden hadn't tricked her. And how frightened she was when she saw that the basket was full – of birch leaves! In anger she threw out two handfuls of leaves, and she was going to shake the entire basket out, but then she bethought herself, 'I will use them as litter for the goats,' and left some leaves in the basket. She was almost afraid to go home.

Her mother was waiting for her on the threshold,

full of anxiety. "For heaven's sake, girl! What sort of spool did you bring me home yesterday?" were her first words.

"Why?" asked Betty anxiously.

"When you went out in the morning, I went to reel. I reeled and reeled, and the spool still remained full. One skein, two, three skeins, the spool still full.

"'What evil spirit has spun it?' said I in a temper, and that instant the yarn vanished from the spindle, as if it were spirited away. Tell me what the meaning of this is!"

Then Betty confessed, and began to tell about the beautiful maiden.

"That was a wood-fairy!" cried her mother in astonishment. "About midday and midnight the wood-ladies hold their dances. Lucky that you are not a boy, or you wouldn't have come out of her arms alive. She would have danced with you as long as there was breath in your body, or have tickled you to death. But they have compassion on girls, and

110

often give them rich presents. It's a shame that you didn't tell me about your meeting her. If I hadn't spoken in a temper, I might have had a whole room full of yarn."

Then Betty bethought herself of the basket, and it occurred to her that perhaps, after all, there might have been something under those leaves. She took out the spindle and unspun flax from the top, and looked once more, and, "See, mother!" she cried out. Her mother looked and clapped her hands. The birch leaves were turned into gold!

"She ordered me, 'Don't look now, but at home!' but I did not obey."

"Lucky that you didn't empty out the whole basket," said her mother. The next morning she went herself to look at the place where Betty had thrown out the two handfuls of leaves, but on the road there lay nothing but fresh birch leaves. But the riches that Betty had brought home were large enough. Her mother bought a small estate, and they had many cattle. Betty had handsome clothes, and was not obliged to pasture goats. But whatever she had, however cheerful and happy she was, nothing ever gave her so great delight as the dance with the wood-lady. She often went to the birch wood. She hoped for the good fortune of seeing the beautiful maiden – but she never set eyes on her again.

Eva's Visit to Fairyland

By Louisa M Alcott

Down among the grass and fragrant clover lay little Eva by the brook-side, watching the bright waves, as they went singing by under the drooping flowers that grew on its banks. As she was wondering where the waters went, she heard a faint, low sound, as of far-off music. She thought it was the wind, but not a leaf was stirring, and soon through the rippling water came a strange little boat.

It was a lily of the valley, whose tall stem formed the mast, while the broad leaves that rose from the roots, and drooped again till they reached the water, were filled with fairies, who danced to the music of the silver lily-bells above that rang a merry peal, and filled the air with their fragrant breath.

Eva's Visit to Fairyland

On came the fairy boat till it reached a moss-grown rock, and here it stopped, while the fairies rested beneath the violet leaves, and sang with the dancing waves.

Eva looked with wonder and threw crimson fruit for the little folks to feast upon.

They looked kindly on the child, and, after whispering long among themselves, two little bright-eyed elves flew over the shining water, and, lighting on the clover blossoms, said gently, "Little maiden, many thanks for your kindness, our queen bids us ask if you will go with us to Fairyland, and learn what we can teach you."

"I would go with you, dear fairies," said Eva, "but I cannot sail in your little boat. See! I can hold you in my hand, and could not live among you without harming your tiny kingdom, I am so large."

The elves laughed, saying, "You are a good child to fear doing harm to those weaker than yourself. Look in the water and see what we have done."

Eva looked into the brook, and saw a tiny child standing between the elves. "Now I can go with you," said she, "but I can no longer step from the bank to yonder stone, for the brook seems now like a great river, and you have not given me wings like yours."

But the fairies took each a hand, and flew lightly over the stream. The queen and her subjects came to meet her. "Now must we go home," said the queen, "and you shall go with us, little one."

Then there was a great bustle, as they flew about on shining wings, some laying cushions of violet leaves in the boat, others folding the queen's veil and mantle more closely round her, lest the falling dews should chill her.

The cool waves' gentle splashing against the boat, and the sweet chime of the lily-bells, lulled little Eva to sleep, and when she woke it was in Fairyland. A faint, rosy light, as of the setting sun, shone on the white pillars of the queen's palace as they passed in. They led Eva to a bed of pure white leaves, above which drooped the fragrant petals of a crimson rose.

With the sun rose the fairies, and, with Eva, hastened away to the fountain, whose cool waters were soon filled with little forms, as the elves floated in the blue waves among the fair white lilies, or sat on the green moss, smoothing their bright locks, and wearing fresh garlands of dewy flowers. Then they flew away to the gardens, and soon, high up among the treetops, or under the broad leaves, sat the elves in little groups, taking their breakfast of fruit and pure fresh dew, while the bright-winged birds came fearlessly among them, pecking the same ripe berries, and dipping their little beaks in the same flower cups.

"Now, little Eva," said they, "you will see that Fairies are not idle, wilful spirits, as mortals believe. Come, we will show you what we do."

They led her to a lovely room, through whose walls of deep green leaves the light stole softly in. Here lay many wounded insects, and creatures, and pale, drooping flowers grew beside urns of healing herbs, from whose fresh leaves came a faint, sweet perfume.

Eva wondered, but silently followed her guide, little Rose-Leaf, who went to the insects – first to a tiny fly who lay in a flower-leaf cradle.

"Do you suffer much, dear Gauzy-Wing?" asked the Fairy. "I will bind up your poor little leg." So she folded the cool leaves tenderly about the poor fly, bathed his wings, and brought him refreshing drink, while he hummed his thanks, and forgot his pain.

They passed on, and Eva saw beside each bed a fairy, who with gentle hands and loving words soothed the suffering insects.

Then Rose-Leaf led Eva away, saying, "Come now to the Flower Palace, and see the Fairy Court."

Beneath green arches, bright with birds and flowers, went Eva into a lofty hall. The roof of pure white lilies rested on pillars of green clustering vines, while many-coloured blossoms threw their bright shadows on the walls, as they danced below in the deep green moss.

Suddenly the music grew louder and sweeter, and the fairies knelt, and bowed their heads, as on through the crowd of loving subjects came the queen, while the air was filled with gay voices singing to welcome her.

She placed the child beside her, saying, "Little Eva, you shall see now how the flowers on your great earth bloom so brightly. A band of loving little gardeners go daily forth from Fairyland, to tend and watch them. Now, Eglantine, what have you to tell us of your rosy namesakes on the earth?"

From a group of elves, whose rose-wreathed wands showed the flower they loved, came one bearing a tiny urn, and, answering the queen, she said, "Over hill and valley they are blooming fresh and fair as summer sun and dew can make them and this, the loveliest of their sisters, have I brought to place among the fairy flowers that never pass away."

Eglantine then laid the urn before the queen, and placed the fragrant rose on the dewy moss beside the throne, while a murmur of approval went around the hall, and each wand in turn waved to the little fairy who could bring so fair a gift to their good queen.

Said little Rose-Leaf to Eva, "Come now and see where we are taught to read the tales written on flower-leaves, and the sweet language of the birds, and all that can make a fairy heart wiser and better."

Then into a cheerful place they went, with many groups of flowers, and among the leaves sat child elves, and learned from their flower-books all that fairy hands had written there. Some studied when to spread tender buds to the sunlight, and when to shelter them from rain, how to guard the seeds, and when to lay them in the warm earth or send them on the summer wind to far off hills and valleys. Others learned to heal wounded insects, who, were it not for fairy hands, would die before half their

120

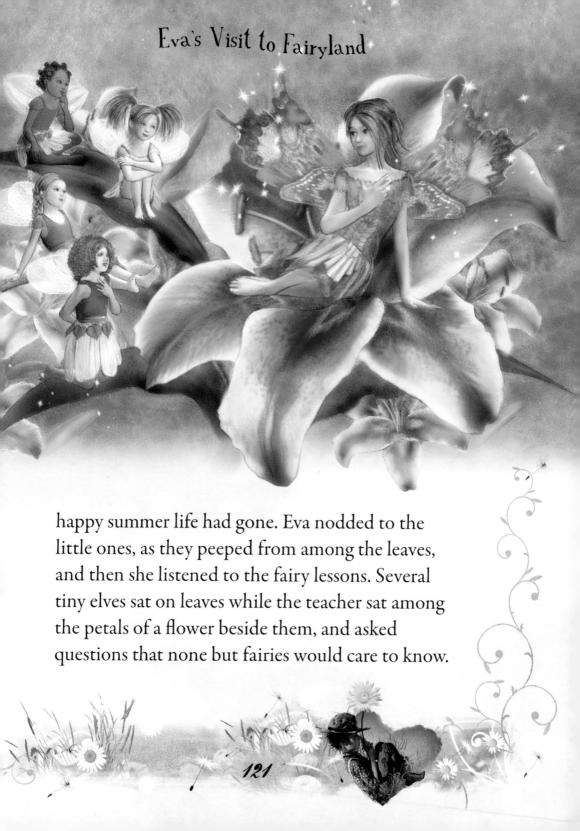

Eva's Visit to Fairyland

happy summer life had gone. Eva nodded to the
little ones, as they peeped from among the leaves,
and then she listened to the fairy lessons. Several
tiny elves sat on leaves while the teacher sat among
the petals of a flower beside them, and asked
questions that none but fairies would care to know.

"Twinkle, if there lay nine seeds within a flower cup and the wind bore five away, how many would the blossom have?"

"Four," replied the little one.

"Rosebud, if a cowslip opens three leaves in one day and four the next, how many rosy leaves will there be when the whole flower has bloomed?"

"Seven," sang the gay little elf.

"Harebell, if a silkworm spins one yard of fairy cloth in an hour, how many will it spin in a day?"

"Twelve," said the fairy child.

"Primrose, where lies Violet Island?"

"In the Lake of Ripples."

"Lilla, what are the bounds of Rose Land?"

"On the north by Ferndale, south by Sunny Wave River, east by the hill of Morning Clouds, and west by the Evening Star."

"Now, little ones," said the teacher, "you may go to your painting."

Then Eva saw how, on large, white leaves, the

Eva's Visit to Fairyland

fairies learned to imitate the lovely colours, and with tiny brushes to brighten the blush on the anemone's cheek, to deepen the blue of the violet's eye, and add new light to the golden cowslip.

"You have stayed long enough," said the elves at length, "we have many things to show you. Come now and see what is our dearest work."

So Eva said farewell to the child elves, and hastened with little Rose-Leaf to the gates. Here she saw many bands of fairies, folded in dark mantles that mortals might not know them, who, with the child among them, flew away over hill and valley. Some went to the cottages amid the hills, some to the seaside to watch above the humble fisher folks, but little Rose-Leaf and many others went into the noisy city.

Eva wondered within herself what good the tiny elves could do in this great place, but she soon learned, for the fairy band went among the poor and friendless, bringing pleasant dreams to the sick and old, sweet, tender thoughts of love and gentleness to the young, strength to the weak, and patient cheerfulness to the poor and lonely.

Thus to all who needed help or comfort went the faithful fairies, and when at length they turned towards Fairyland, many were the grateful, happy hearts they left behind.

All Fairyland was dressed in flowers, and the soft wind went singing by, laden with their fragrant breath. Sweet music sounded through the air, and troops of elves in their gayest robes hastened to the palace where the feast was spread.

Soon the hall was filled with smiling faces and fair forms, and little Eva, as she stood beside the queen, thought she had never seen a sight so lovely.

The many-coloured shadows of the fairest flowers played on the pure white walls, and fountains sparkled in the sunlight, making music as the cool waves rose and fell, while to and fro, with waving wings and joyous voices, went the smiling elves, bearing fruit and honey, or fragrant garlands for each other's hair.

Long they feasted, gaily they sang, and Eva, dancing merrily among them, longed to be an elf that she might dwell forever in so fair a home.

At length the music ceased, and the queen said, as she laid her hand on little Eva's shining hair, "Dear child, tomorrow we must bear you home, therefore we will guide you to the brook-side, and there say farewell till you come again to visit us. Nay, do not weep, dear Rose-Leaf, you shall watch over little Eva's flowers, and when she looks at them she will think of you. Come now and lead her to the fairy garden, and show her what we think our fairest sight."

With Rose-Leaf by her side, they led her through the palace, and along green, winding paths, till Eva saw what seemed a wall of flowers before her, while the air was filled with the most fragrant odours, and the low, sweet music as of singing blossoms.

"Where have you brought me, and what mean these lovely sounds?" asked Eva.

"Look here, and you shall see," said Rose-Leaf, as she bent aside the vines, "but listen silently or you cannot hear."

Then Eva, looking through the drooping vines, beheld a garden filled with the loveliest flowers. Fair as were all the blossoms she had seen in Fairyland, none were so beautiful as these. The rose glowed with a deeper crimson, the lily's soft leaves were more purely white, the crocus and humble cowslip shone like sunlight, and the violet was blue as the sky that smiled above it.

"How beautiful they are," whispered Eva, "but, dear Rose-Leaf, why do you keep them here, and why call you this your fairest sight?"

"Look again, and I will tell you," said the fairy.

Eva looked, and saw from every flower a tiny form come forth to welcome the elves, who all, save Rose-Leaf, had flown above the wall, and were now scattering dew upon the flowers' bright leaves and talking gaily with the spirits, who gathered around them, and seemed full of joy that they had come. The child saw that each one wore the colours of the flower that was its home. Delicate and graceful were the little forms, bright the silken hair that fell about each lovely face, and Eva heard the low, sweet murmur of their silvery voices and the rustle of their wings. She gazed in silent wonder, forgetting she knew not who they were, till the fairy said, "These are the spirits of the flowers, and this the fairy home where they come to bloom in fadeless beauty here, when their earthly life is past. Come now, for you have seen enough. We must be away."

On a rosy morning cloud, went Eva through the sunny sky. The fresh wind bore them gently on, and soon they stood again beside the brook, whose waves danced brightly as if to welcome them.

"Now, we say farewell," said the queen, as they gathered nearer to the child.

They clung about her tenderly, and little Rose-Leaf placed a flower crown on her head, whispering softly, "When you would come to us again, stand by the brook-side and wave this in the air, and we will gladly take you to our home again. Farewell, dear Eva. Think of your little Rose-Leaf when among the flowers."

For a long time Eva watched their shining wings, and listened to the music of their voices as they flew singing home, and when at length the last little form had vanished among the clouds, she saw that all around her where the elves

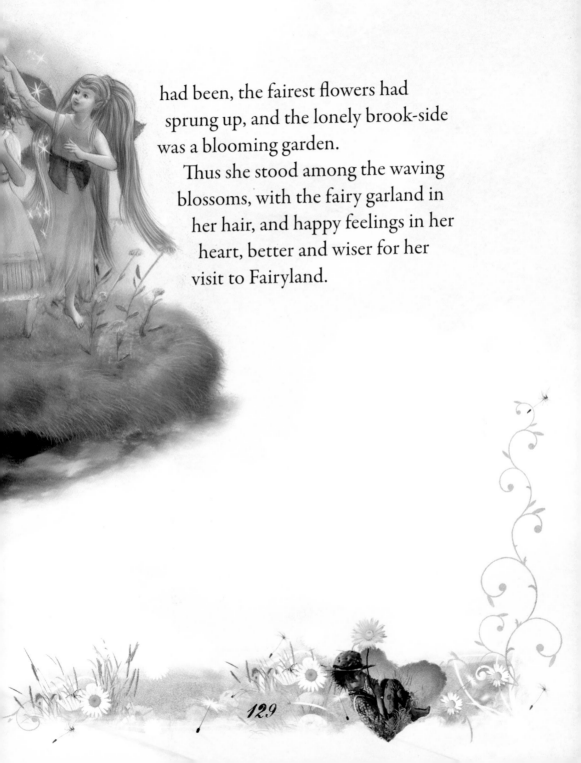

Eva's Visit to Fairyland

had been, the fairest flowers had
sprung up, and the lonely brook-side
was a blooming garden.

Thus she stood among the waving
blossoms, with the fairy garland in
her hair, and happy feelings in her
heart, better and wiser for her
visit to Fairyland.

The Counterpane Fairy

By Katharine Pyle

*T*eddy was all alone, for his mother had been up
with him so much the night before that at
four o'clock in the afternoon she said that she was
going to lie down.

She set a glass of milk on his bedside table, and
left the door ajar so that he could call the cook if he
wanted anything, and then she had gone to bed.

The little boy usually quite liked being ill, for

then he was read aloud to and had lemonade, but this had been a real illness, and though he was better now, he was still only allowed milk and gruel. He was feeling rather lonely, too, though the fire crackled cheerfully, and he could hear Hannah singing to herself in the kitchen below.

He lay staring out of the window at the grey clouds sweeping across the sky. He grew lonelier and lonelier and a big tear trickled down his cheek and dripped off his chin.

"Oh dear, oh dear!" said a little voice just behind the hill his knees made as he sat with them drawn up in bed, "What a hill to climb!"

Teddy stopped crying and gazed wonderingly at where the voice came from, and over the top of his knees appeared a brown peaked hood, a tiny withered face, a brown cloak, and last of all two small feet in buckled shoes. It was a little old woman, so weazened and brown that she looked more like a dried leaf than anything else.

She seated herself on Teddy's knees and gazed at him solemnly, and she was so light that he felt her weight no more than if she had been a feather.

Teddy stared at her for a while, and then he asked, "Who are you?"

"I'm the Counterpane Fairy," said the little

The Counterpane Fairy

figure, in a thin little voice. "I came to you, because you were lonely and sick, and I thought maybe you would like me to show you a story."

"Do you mean tell me a story?" asked Teddy.

"No," said the fairy, "I mean show you a story. It's a game I invented after I joined the Counterpane Fairies. Choose any one of the squares of the counterpane and I will show you how to play it. That's all you have to do – choose a square."

Teddy looked the counterpane over carefully. "I think I'll choose that yellow square," he said, "because it looks so nice and bright."

"Very well," said the Counterpane Fairy. "Look straight at it and don't turn away until I count seven times seven and then you shall see the story of it."

Teddy fixed his eyes on the square and the fairy began to count. "One – two – three – four," she counted, Teddy heard her voice, thin and clear as the hissing of the logs on the hearth. "Don't look away from the square," she cried. "Five – six –

seven," it seemed to Teddy that the yellow silk square was turning to a mist before his eyes and wrapping everything about him in a golden glow. "Thirteen – fourteen," the fairy counted on and on. "Forty-six – forty-seven – forty-eight – *forty nine*!"

At the words 'forty-nine', the Counterpane Fairy clapped her hands and Teddy looked about him. He was no longer in a golden mist. He was standing in a wonderful enchanted garden. The sky was like the golden sky at sunset, and the grass was so thickly set with tiny yellow flowers that it looked like a golden carpet. From this garden stretched a long flight of glass steps. They reached up and up and up to a great golden castle with shining domes and turrets.

"Listen!" said the Counterpane Fairy. "In that golden castle there lies an enchanted princess. For more than a hundred years she has been lying there waiting for the hero who is to come and rescue her, and you are the hero who can do it if you will."

With that the fairy led him to a little pool close

by, and bade him look in the water. When Teddy looked, he saw himself standing there in the golden garden, and he did not appear as he ever had before. He was tall and strong and beautiful, like a hero.

"Yes," said Teddy, "I will do it." Without further pause, he ran to the glass steps and began to climb.

Up and up and up he went. Once he turned and waved his hand to the Counterpane Fairy in the golden garden below. She waved her hand, and he heard her voice faint and clear, "Goodbye! Be brave and strong, and beware of what is little and grey."

Then Teddy turned towards the castle, and in a moment he was standing before the shining gates.

He raised his hand and struck bravely upon the door. There was no answer. Again he struck upon it, and his blow rang through the hall inside. Then he opened the door and went in.

The hall was five-sided, and all of pure gold, as clear and shining as glass. Upon three sides of it were three arched doors – one was of emerald, one was of ruby, and one was of diamond. They were arched, and tall, and wide – fit for a hero to go through. The question was, behind which one lay the enchanted princess?

While Teddy stood there looking at them and wondering, he heard a little thin voice, that seemed to be singing to itself, and this is what it sang:

> *"In and out and out and in,*
> *Quick as a flash I weave and spin.*
> *Some may mistake and some forget,*
> *But I'll have my spider web finished yet."*

When Teddy heard the song, he knew that someone must be awake in the enchanted castle, so he began looking about him.

On the fourth side of the wall there hung a curtain of silvery-grey spider web, and the voice seemed to come from it. The hero went towards it, but he saw nothing, for the spider that was spinning

"In and out and out and in,

Quick as a flash I weave and spin.

Some may mistake and some forget,

But I'll have my spider web finished yet."

it moved so fast that no eyes could follow it.
Presently it paused up in the corner of the web, and
then Teddy saw it. It looked very little to have spun
all that curtain of silvery web.

"Mistress Spinner!" cried Teddy. "Can you tell
me where to find the enchanted princess who lies
asleep waiting for me to rescue her?"

The spider sat quite still for a while, and then it
said in a voice as thin as a hair:

> *"You must go through the emerald door,*
> *You must go through the emerald door.*
> *What so fit as the emerald door,*
> *For the hero who would do great deeds?"*

Teddy did not so much as stay to thank the little
grey spinner, he was in such a hurry to find the
princess, but turning he sprang to the emerald door,
flung it open, and stepped outside.

He found himself standing on the glass steps,

and as his foot touched the topmost one the whole flight closed up like an umbrella, and in a moment Teddy was sliding down the smooth glass pane, faster and faster and faster until he could hardly catch his breath.

The next thing he knew he was standing in the golden garden, and there was the Counterpane Fairy beside him looking at him sadly. "You should have known better than to try the emerald door," she said, "and now shall we break the story?"

"Oh, no, no!" cried Teddy, and he was still the hero. "Let me try once more, for it may be I can yet save the princess."

The Counterpane Fairy smiled. "Very well," she said. "Try again. But remember what I told you: beware of what is little and grey, and take this with you – it may be of use." She picked up a blade of grass from the ground and handed it to him.

The hero took it, and in his hands it changed to a sword that shone so brightly that it dazzled his eyes.

Then he turned, and there was the long flight of glass steps leading up to the golden castle just as before, so thrusting the sword into his belt, he ran nimbly up and up. When he reached the topmost step he waved farewell to the Counterpane Fairy below. She waved her hand to him. "Remember," she called, "beware of what is little and grey."

He opened the door and went into the five-sided golden hall, and there were the three doors just as before, and the spider spinning on the fourth side:

"Now the brave hero is wiser indeed,
He may have failed once, but he still may succeed.
Dull are the emeralds, diamonds are bright,
So is his wisdom that shines as the light."

"The diamond door!" cried Teddy. "Yes, that is the door that I should have tried. How could I have thought the emerald door was it?" And opening the diamond door he stepped through it.

The Counterpane Fairy

He hardly had time to see that he was standing at the top of the glass steps, before – *brrrr!* – they had shut up again into a smooth glass hill, and there he was spinning down them so fast that the wind whistled past his ears.

In less time than it takes to tell, he was back again for the third time in the golden garden, with the Counterpane Fairy standing before him, and he was ashamed to raise his eyes.

"So!" said the Counterpane Fairy. "Did you know no better than to open the diamond door?"

"No," said Teddy, "I knew no better."

"Then," said the fairy, "if you can pay no better heed to my warnings than that, the princess must wait for another hero, for you are not the one."

"Let me try but once more," cried Teddy, "for this time I shall surely find her."

"Then you may try once more and for the last time," said the fairy, "but beware of what is little and grey." Stooping she picked from the grass beside

141

her a fallen acorn cup and handed it to him. "Take this with you," she said, "for it may serve you well."

As he took it from her, it was changed in his hand to a goblet of gold set round with precious stones. Turning he ran for the third time up the flight of glass steps. All the time he ran he was wondering what the fairy meant about her warning. She had said, 'Beware of what is little and grey.' What had he seen that was little and grey?

When he reached the golden hall the spider was spinning fast, but presently it stopped up in the corner of the web. As the hero looked at it he saw that it was little and grey. Then it began to sing to him in its tiny thin voice:

"Great hero, wiser than ever before,
Try the red door, try the red door.
Open the door that is ruby, and then
You never need search for the princess again."

"No, I will not open the ruby door," cried Teddy. "I have followed your instructions twice and both times you have you sent me back to the golden garden, and now you shall fool me no more."

As he said this he saw that a corner of the web was unfinished, and underneath was something that looked like a little yellow door. Suddenly he knew that this was the door he must go through. He pulled at the curtain of web but it was as strong as steel. Quickly he snatched from his belt the magic sword, and with one blow the curtain was cut in two, and fell at his feet.

He heard the spider calling to him but paid no heed, for he had opened the door and stooped his head and entered.

Beyond was a great gold courtyard with a fountain splashing into a golden basin in the middle. But what he saw first was the princess, who lay stretched out as if asleep upon a couch all covered with cloth of gold.

He knew she was a princess, because she was so beautiful and because she wore a delicate crown.

He stood looking at her without stirring, and at last he whispered, "Princess! Princess! I have come to save you."

Still she did not stir. He bent and touched her, but she lay there in her enchanted sleep, and her eyes did not open. Then Teddy looked about him, and seeing the fountain he drew the magic cup from his bosom and, filling it, sprinkled the hands and face of the princess with the water.

Then her eyes opened and she raised herself upon her elbow and smiled. "Have you come at last?" she cried.

"Yes," answered Teddy, "I have come."

The princess looked about her. "But what became of the spider?" she said. Then Teddy, too, looked about, and there was the spider running across the floor towards where the princess lay. Quickly he sprang from her side and set his foot upon it. There was a thin squeak and then – there was nothing left of the little grey spinner but a tiny grey smudge on the floor.

Instantly the golden castle was shaken from top to bottom, and there was a sound of many voices shouting outside. The princess rose to her feet and caught the hero by the hand. "You have broken the enchantment," she cried, "and now you shall be the king of the golden castle and reign with me."

"Oh, but I can't," said Teddy, "because, because–"

But the princess drew him out with her through the hall, and there they were at the head of the flight of glass steps. A great host of soldiers and courtiers were running up it. They were dressed in cloth of gold, and they shouted at the sight of Teddy, "Hail to the hero! Hail to the hero!"

"And all this is yours," said the beautiful princess, turning towards him with—

"So that is the story of the yellow square," said the Counterpane Fairy.

Teddy looked about him. The golden castle had vanished, and the stairs, and the shouting courtiers. He was lying in bed with the coverlet over his knees and Hannah was still singing in the kitchen below.

"Did you like it?" asked the fairy.

Teddy heaved a deep sigh. "Oh! Wasn't it beautiful?" he said. Then he lay for a while thinking and smiling. "Wasn't the princess lovely?" he whispered half to himself.

The Counterpane Fairy got up slowly and stiffly,

and picked up the staff that she had laid down beside her. "Well, I must be journeying on," she said.

"Oh, no, no!" cried Teddy. "Please don't go yet."

"Yes, I must," said the Counterpane Fairy. "I hear your mother coming."

"But will you come back again?" cried Teddy.

The Counterpane Fairy made no answer. She was walking down the other side of the bed-quilt hill, and Teddy heard her voice, little and thin, dying away in the distance, "Oh dear, dear, dear! What a hill to go down! What a hill! Oh dear, dear, dear!"

Then the door opened and his mother came in. She was looking rested, and she smiled at him lovingly, but the little brown Counterpane Fairy was gone.

148

FAIRY
HELPERS

Mrs Bedonebyasyoudid and Mrs Doasyouwouldbedoneby

From *The Water Babies* by Charles Kingsley

Tom is a chimney-sweep's boy who has run away from his cruel master. When he tried to wash away his soot in a stream, he fell in and became a water baby. He has been swimming around on his own for some time.

And now a wonderful thing happened to Tom – he came upon a water baby.

A real live water baby, sitting on the white sand, very busy about a little point of rock. And when it saw Tom it looked up for a moment, and then cried, "Why, you are not one of us. You are a new baby!

Mrs Bedonebyasyoudid and Mrs Doasyouwouldbedoneby

Oh, how delightful!"

Tom looked at the baby again, and then he said, "Well, this is wonderful! I have seen things just like you again and again, but I thought you were shells, or sea creatures. I never took you for water babies like myself."

"Now," said the baby, "come and help me, or I shall not have finished before my brothers and sisters come, and it is time to go home."

"What shall I help you at?"

"At this poor dear little rock. A great clumsy boulder came rolling by in the last storm, and knocked all its head off, and rubbed off all its flowers. And now I must plant it again with seaweeds, coral and anemones, and I will make it the prettiest rock garden on all the shore."

So they worked away at the rock, and planted it, and smoothed the sand down round it, and capital fun they had till the tide began to turn. And then Tom heard all the other babies coming, laughing and singing and shouting and romping, and the noise they made was just like the noise of the ripple. And in they came, dozens and dozens of them, some bigger than Tom and some smaller, all in the neatest little white bathing dresses, and when they found that he was a new baby, they hugged him and kissed him, and then put him in the middle and danced round him on the sand, and there was no one ever so happy as poor little Tom.

"Now then," they cried all at once, "we must come away home, we must come away home, or the tide will leave us dry. We have mended all the broken seaweed, and put all the rock-pools in order, and planted all the shells again in the sand, and nobody will see where the ugly storm swept in last week."

And this is the reason why the rock-pools are always so neat and clean – because the water babies come inshore after every storm to sweep them out, and comb them down, and put them all to rights again.

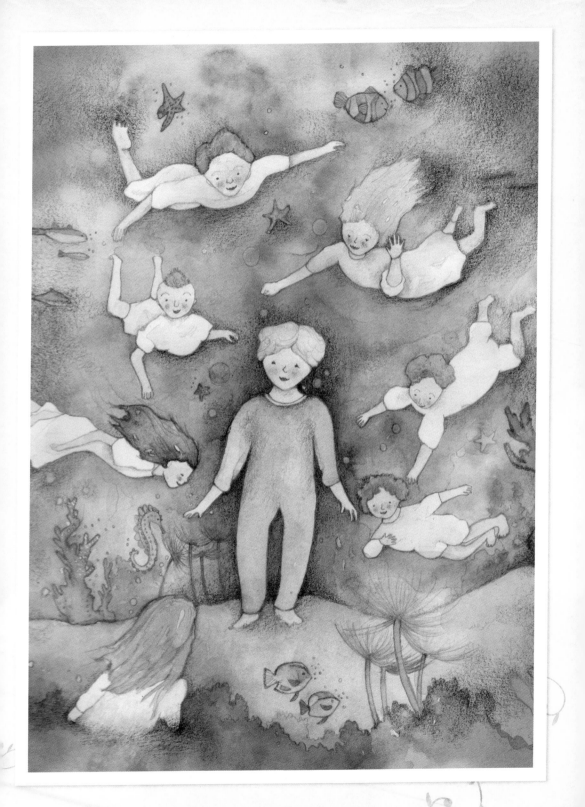

FAIRY HELPERS

Only where men are wasteful and dirty, and let sewers run into the sea instead of putting the stuff upon the fields like thrifty reasonable souls, or throw herrings' heads and dead dog-fish, or any other refuse, into the water, or in any way make a mess upon the clean shore – only there the water babies will not come, sometimes not for hundreds of years (for they cannot abide anything smelly or foul). Instead they leave the sea anemones and the crabs to clear away everything, and after a time the good tidy sea covers up all the dirt in soft mud and clean sand.

And where is the home of the water babies? In St Brandan's fairy isle.

Did you never hear of the blessed St Brandan, who far away, before the setting sun, saw a blue fairy sea, and golden fairy islands, and he said, "Those are the islands of the blest." Then he and his friends got into a boat, and sailed away and away to the westward, and were never heard of again.

Mrs Bedonebyasyoudid and Mrs Doasyouwouldbedoneby

And when St Brandan and the hermits came to that fairy isle they found it overgrown with cedars and full of beautiful birds, and he sat down under the cedars and preached to all the birds in the air. And they liked his sermons so well that they told the fishes in the sea, and they came, and St Brandan preached to them. And the fishes told the water babies, who live in the caves under the isle, and they came up by hundreds.

He taught the water babies for a great many hundred years, until his eyes grew too dim to see, and his beard grew so long that he dared not walk for fear of treading on it, and then he might have tumbled down. And at last he and the five hermits fell fast asleep under the shade of the cedars, and there they sleep unto this day. So then the fairies took to the water babies, and taught them their lessons themselves.

And on still clear summer evenings, when the sun sinks down into the sea, among the golden cloud-capes and cloud-islands, and locks and friths of azure sky, the sailors fancy that they see, away to westward, St Brandan's fairy isle.

Now when Tom got there, he found that the isle stood all on pillars, and that its roots were full of caves all curtained and draped with seaweeds, purple and crimson, green and brown, and strewn with soft white sand, on which the water babies sleep every night. But, to keep the place clean and sweet, the crabs picked up all the scraps off the floor and ate them like so many monkeys, while the rocks were covered with ten thousand sea anemones, and corals, who scavenged the water all day long, and kept it nice and pure.

But I wish Tom had given up all his naughty tricks, and left off tormenting dumb animals now that he had plenty of playfellows to amuse him. Instead of that, I am sorry to say, he would meddle with the creatures, all but the water-snakes, for they would stand no nonsense.

Mrs Bedonebyasyoudid and
Mrs Doasyouwouldbedoneby

So he frightened the crabs, to make them hide in the sand and peep out at him with the tips of their eyes, and put stones into the anemones' mouths, to make them fancy that their dinner was coming.

The other children warned him, and said, "Take care what you are at. Mrs Bedonebyasyoudid is coming." But Tom never listened to them, being quite riotous with high spirits and good luck, till, one Friday morning early, Mrs Bedonebyasyoudid came indeed.

FAIRY HELPERS

A very tremendous lady she was, and when the children saw her they all stood in a row, very upright indeed, and smoothed down their bathing dresses, and put their hands behind their backs – it was just as if they were all going to be examined by the inspector.

And she had on a black bonnet, and a black shawl, and a pair of large green spectacles, and a great hooked nose, hooked so much that the bridge of it stood quite up above her eyebrows, and under her arm she carried a great birch-rod. Indeed, she was so ugly that Tom was tempted to make faces at her – but did not, for he did not admire the look of the birch-rod under her arm.

And she looked at the children one by one, and seemed very much pleased with them, though she never asked them one question about how they were behaving, and then began giving them all sorts of nice sea-things – sea-cakes, sea-apples, sea-oranges, sea-bullseyes, sea-toffee, and to the very best of all she gave sea-ices, made out of sea-cows' cream, which never melt under water.

And, if you don't quite believe me, then just think – what is more cheap and plentiful than sea-rock? Then why should there not be sea-toffee as well? And every one can find sea-lemons (ready quartered too) if they will look for them at low tide, and sea-grapes too sometimes, hanging in bunches. Now little Tom watched all these sweet things given away, till his mouth watered, and his eyes grew as round as an owl's. For he hoped that his turn would come at last, and so it did. For the lady called him up, and held out her fingers with something in them, and popped it into his mouth – and, lo and behold, it was a nasty cold hard pebble.

"You are a very cruel woman," said he, and began to whimper.

"And you are a very cruel boy, who puts pebbles into the sea anemones' mouths, to take them in, and make them fancy that they had caught a good dinner! As you did to them, so I must do to you."

"Who told you that?" said Tom.

"You did yourself, this very minute."

Tom had never opened his lips, so he was very much taken aback indeed.

"Yes, everyone tells me exactly what they have done wrong, and that without knowing it themselves. So there is no use trying to hide anything from me. Now go, and be a good boy, and I will put no more pebbles in your mouth, if you put none in other creatures.'"

"I did not know there was any harm in it," said Tom.

Mrs Bedonebyasyoudid and
Mrs Doasyouwouldbedoneby

"Then you know now."

"Well, you are a little hard on a poor lad," said Tom, reproachfully.

"Not at all – I am the best friend you ever had in all your life. But I will tell you, I cannot help punishing people when they do wrong. I like it no more than they do. I am often very, very sorry for them, poor things, but I cannot help it. If I tried not to do it, I should do it all the same. For I work by machinery, just like an engine, and am full of wheels and springs inside, and am wound up very carefully, so that I cannot help going."

"Was it long ago since they wound you up?" asked Tom. For he thought, the cunning little fellow, 'She will run down some day, or they may forget to wind her up.'

"I was wound up once and for all, so long ago, that I forget all about it."

"You must have been made a long time!" exclaimed Tom.

"I never was made, my child, and I shall go forever and ever, for I am as old as Eternity, and yet as young as Time."

And there came over the lady's face a very curious expression – very solemn, and very sad, and yet very, very sweet. And she looked up and away, as if she were gazing through the sea, and through the sky, at something far, far off, and as she did so, there came such a quiet, tender, patient, hopeful smile over her face that Tom thought for the moment that she did not look ugly at all.

And Tom smiled in her face, she looked so pleasant for the moment. And the strange fairy smiled too, and said, "Yes. You thought me very ugly just now, did you not?"

Tom hung down his head, and got very red about the ears.

"And I am very ugly. I am the ugliest fairy in the world, and I shall be, till people behave themselves as they ought to do. And then I shall grow as

Mrs Bedonebyasyoudid and Mrs Doasyouwouldbedoneby

handsome as my sister – the loveliest fairy in the world. Her name is Mrs Doasyouwouldbedoneby. So she begins where I end, and I begin where she ends, and those who will not listen to her must listen to me, as you will see."

Poor old Mrs Bedonebyasyoudid! She has a great deal of hard work before her, and had better have been born a washerwoman, and stood over a tub all day. But, you see, people cannot always choose their own profession.

Tom determined to be a very good boy all Saturday, and he was, for he never frightened one crab, nor tickled any live corals, nor put stones into the sea anemones' mouths, to make them fancy they had got a dinner. And when Sunday morning came, sure enough, Mrs Doasyouwouldbedoneby came too. Whereat all the little children began dancing and clapping their hands and Tom danced too with all his might.

And as for the pretty lady, I cannot tell you what

163

the colour of her hair was, or of her eyes. No more
could Tom, for, when anyone looks at her, all they
can think of is that she has the sweetest, kindest,
tenderest, funniest, merriest face they ever saw, or
want to see. But Tom saw that she was a very tall
woman, as tall as her sister. But instead of being
gnarly and horny, and scaly, and prickly, like her, she
was the most nice, soft, fat, smooth, cuddly creature
who ever nursed a baby, and she understood babies
thoroughly, for she had plenty of her own, whole
rows and regiments of them, and has to this day.

And all her delight was, whenever she had a spare
moment, to play with babies, in which she showed
herself a woman of sense, for babies are the best
company, and the pleasantest playfellows in the
world, at least, so all the wise people in the world
think. And therefore when the children saw her,
they naturally all caught hold of her, and pulled her
till she sat down on a stone, and climbed into her
lap, and clung round her neck, and caught hold of

her hands. And then they all put their thumbs into their mouths, and began cuddling and purring like so many kittens, as they ought to have done. While those who could get nowhere else sat down on the sand, and cuddled her feet – for no one, you know, wears shoes in the water. And Tom stood staring, for he could not understand what it was all about.

"And who are you, you little darling?" she said.

"Oh, that is the new baby!" they all cried, pulling their thumbs out of their mouths, "And he never had any mother," and they all put their thumbs back again, for they did not wish to lose any time.

"Then I will be his mother, and he shall have the very best place, so get out, all of you, this moment."

And she took up two great armfuls of babies – nine hundred under one arm, and thirteen hundred under the other – and threw them away, right and left, into the water. But they did not even take their thumbs out of their mouths, but came paddling and wriggling back to her like so many tadpoles.

FAIRY HELPERS

But she took Tom in her arms, and laid him in the softest place of all, and kissed him, and patted him, and talked to him, tenderly and low, such

Mrs Bedonebyasyoudid and
Mrs Doasyouwouldbedoneby

things as he had never heard before in his life, and
Tom looked up into her eyes, and loved her, and
loved, till he fell fast asleep from pure love.

And when he woke she was telling the children a
story. And what story did she tell them? One story
she told them, which begins every Christmas Eve,
and yet never ends at all forever and ever. And, as
she went on, the children took their thumbs out of
their mouths and listened quite seriously, but not
sadly at all, for she never told them anything sad,
and Tom listened too, and never grew tired of
listening. And he listened so long that he fell fast
asleep again, and, when he woke, the lady was
nursing him still.

"Don't go away," said little Tom. "This is so nice.
I never had any one to cuddle me before."

"Now," said the fairy to Tom, "will you be a good
boy for my sake, and torment no more sea beasts till
I come back?"

"And you will cuddle me again?" said poor Tom.

"Of course I will, you little duck. I should like to take you with me and cuddle you all the way, only I must not," and away she went.

So Tom really tried to be a good boy, and tormented no sea beasts after that as long as he lived, and he is quite alive, I assure you, still.

The Touch of Iron

By William Elliot Griffis

Some people believe the fairies were the original inhabitants of ancient lands before humans came and drove them to hide in caves and wild places. Another common belief is that fairies cannot stand the touch of cold iron. This story uses these two ideas to tell its tale. Cymry is the Welsh word for the inhabitants of Wales.

Ages ago, before the Cymry travelled across the sea, a race of fairies already lived in the Land of Honey, as Great Britain was then called.

These ancient fairies, who lived in caves, did not know how to build houses or to plough the ground.

FAIRY HELPERS

They had no idea that they could get their food out of the earth. As for making bread, pies and goodies, they never heard of such a thing. They did not know how to use fire for melting copper, nor did they know how to get iron from ore to make strong knives and spears, arrow heads and swords, and armour and helmets.

All they could do was mould clay to make things to cook with. When they baked this soft stuff in the fire, they found they had pots, pans and dishes as hard as stone, though these were easily broken.

To hunt the deer, or fight the wolves and bears, they fashioned clubs of wood. For javelins and arrows, they took hard stone like flint and chipped it to points and sharpened it with edges. This was the time which we now call the Stone Age, and when the fairies went to war, their weapons were wholly of wood or stone.

They had not yet learned to weave the wool of the sheep into warm clothing, but they wore the

skins of animals. Each one of the caves in which
they lived was a boarding house for dogs and pigs,
as well as people.

When a young man of one fairy tribe wanted a
wife, he sallied out secretly into another
neighbourhood. There he lay in wait for a girl to
come along. He then ran away with her, and back to
his own daddy's cave.

When the Cymry came into the land, they had
iron tools and better weapons of war. Then there
were many and long battles and the fairies were
beaten many times.

So the fairies hated everything that was made of
iron. Anyone of them, girls or boys, who had picked
up iron ornaments, and were found wearing or
using iron tools, or buying anything of iron from
the cave people's enemies, was looked upon as a
rascal, or a villain, or even as a traitor and was
driven out of the tribe.

However, some of the daughters of the fairies

were so pretty and had such rosy cheeks, and lovely figures, and beautiful, long hair, that quite often the Cymric youth fell in love with them.

Many of the fairy daughters were captured and became wives of the Cymry and mothers of children. Over time, their descendants helped to make the bright, witty, song-loving Welsh people.

Now the fairies usually like things that are old, and they are very slow to alter the ancient customs to which they have been used, for, in the fairy world, there is no measure of time, nor any clocks, watches, or bells to strike the hours, and no calendars to mark the passing of the days.

The fairies cannot understand why ladies change the fashions so often, and the men their ways of doing things. They wonder why beards are fashionable at one time, then moustaches long or short at another, or smooth faces when razors are cheap. Most fairies like to keep on doing the same thing in the old way. They enjoy being like the

The Touch of Iron

mountains, which stand, or the sea, that rolls, or the sun, that rises and sets every day and forever. They never get tired of repeating tomorrow what they did yesterday. They are very different from the people that are always wanting something else.

That is the reason why the fairies did not like iron, or to see men wearing iron hats and clothes, called helmets and armour, when they went to war. They no more wanted to be touched by iron than by filth, or foul disease. They hated knives, stirrups, scythes, swords, pots, pans, kettles, or this metal in any form, whether sheet, barbed wire, lump or pig iron.

Now there was a long, pretty stretch of water, near which lived a handsome lad, who loved nothing better than to go out late on moonlight nights and see the fairies dance, or listen to their music. This youth fell in love with one of these fairies, whose beauty was dazzling beyond description. At last, unable to control his passion, he rushed into the midst of the fairy company,

173

seized the beautiful one, and rushed back to his home, with his prize in his arms. This was in true cave-man fashion.

When the other fairies hurried to rescue her, they found the man's house shut. They dared not touch the door, for it had iron studs and bands, and was bolted with the metal they most abhorred.

The Touch of Iron

The young man immediately began to woo the fairy maid, hoping to win her to be his wife. For a long time she refused, and moped all day and night. While weeping many salt water tears, she declared that she was too homesick to live.

She was a smart fairy, and was sure she could outwit the man, even if he had every sort of iron everywhere in order to keep her as it were in a prison. So, pretending she loved him dearly, she said, "I will not be your wife, but, if you can find out my name, I shall gladly become your servant."

'Easily won,' thought the lover to himself. Yet the game was a harder one to play than he supposed. It was like playing 'Blind Man's Buff', or 'Hunt the Slipper'. Although he made guesses of every name he could think of, he was never 'hot' and got no nearer to the thing sought than if his eyes were bandaged. All the time, he was deeper and deeper in love with the lovely fairy maid.

But one night when he was returning home, he

saw a group of fairies sitting on a log. At once, he thought they might be talking about their lost sister. So he crept up close to them, and soon found that he had guessed right. After a long discussion, finding themselves still at a loss as to how to recover her, he heard one of them sigh and say, "Oh, Siwsi, my sister, how can you live with a mortal?"

"Enough," said the young man to himself. "I've got it." Then, crawling away noiselessly, he ran back all the way to his house, and unlocked the door. Once inside the room, he called out his servant's name, "Siwsi! Siwsi!"

Astonished at hearing her name, she cried out, "What mortal has betrayed me? For, surely no fairy would tell on me? Alas, my fate, my fate!"

But in her own mind, the struggle and the fear were over. She had bravely striven to keep her fairyhood, and in the battle of wits, had lost.

She would not be a wife, but what a wise, superb and faithful servant she made!

The Touch of Iron

Everything prospered under her hand. The house and the farm became models. Not twice, but three times a day, the cows, milked by her, yielded milk unusually rich in cream. In the market, her butter excelled, in quality and price, all others.

In the end, she agreed to become his wife – but only on one condition.

"You must never strike me with iron," she said. "If you do, I'll feel free to leave you, and go back to my relatives in the fairy family."

A hearty laugh from the happy lover greeted this remark. He thought that the condition was very easy to obey.

So they were married, and no couple in all the land seemed happier. Once, twice, the cradle was filled. It rocked with new treasures that had life, and were more dear than farm, or home, or wealth in barns or cattle, cheese and butter. A boy and a girl were theirs. Then the mother's care was contant.

Even though the happy father grew richer every

year, and bought farm after farm until he owned five thousand acres, he valued most his lovely wife and his two beautiful children.

Yet this very delight and affection made him less careful concerning the promise he had once given to his fairy wife, who still held to the ancient ideas of the fairy family in regard to iron.

One of his finest mares had given birth to a filly, which, when the day of the great fair came, he determined to sell at a high price.

So with a halter on his arm, he went out to catch the filly. But she was a spirited creature, so frisky that it was much like his first attempt to win his fairy bride. The lively and frolicsome beast scampered here and there, grazing as she stopped, as if she were determined to put off her capture as long as possible.

So, calling to his wife, the two of them together tried their skill to catch the filly. This time, leaving the halter in the house, the man took bit and bridle,

The Touch of Iron

and the two managed to get the pretty creature into a corner, but, when they had almost captured her, away she dashed again.

By this time, the man was so vexed that he lost his temper, and he who does that, usually loses the game, while he who controls the wrath within, wins. Mad as a flaming fire, he lost his brains also and threw the bit and bridle and the whole harness as far as he could, after the fleeting animal.

Alas! Alas! The wife had started to run after the
filly and the iron bit struck her on the cheek. It did
not hurt, but he had broken his vow.

Now came the surprise of his life. It was as if, at
one moment, a flash of lightning had made all
things bright, and then in another second was inky
darkness. He saw this lovely wife, one moment
active and fleet as a deer. In another, in the
twinkling of an eye, nothing was there. She had
vanished. After this, there was a lonely home, empty
of its light and cheer.

But by living with human beings, a new idea and
form of life had transformed this fairy, and a new
spell was laid on her. Mother-love had been
awakened in her heart. Henceforth, though the law
of the fairy world would not allow her to touch
again the realm of earth, she, having once been wife
and parent, could not forget the babies born of her
body. So, making a grass raft, a floating island, she
came up at night. And often, while these three

mortals lived, this fairy mother would spend hours tenderly talking to her husband and her two children, who were now big boy and girl, as they stood on the lake shore.

Even today, good people sometimes see a little island floating on the lake, and point it out as the place where the fairy mother used to come and talk with her dear ones.

The Phantom Vessel

By Norman Hinsdale Pitman

Once a ship loaded with pleasure seekers was sailing from North China to Shanghai. Stormy weather had delayed her, and she was still one week from port when a great plague broke out on board. The terrible illness attacked passengers and sailors alike until there were so few left to sail the vessel that it seemed as if she would soon be left to the mercy of winds and waves.

The Phantom Vessel

On all sides lay the dead, and the groans of the dying were most terrible to hear. Of that great company of travellers only one, a little boy named Ying-lo, had escaped. At last the few sailors, who had been trying hard to save their ship, were obliged to lie down upon the deck, a prey to the dreadful sickness, and soon they too were dead.

Ying-lo now found himself alone on the sea. For some reason – he did not know why – the gods or the sea fairies had spared him, but as he looked about in terror at the friends and loved ones who had died, he almost wished that he might join them.

The sails flapped about like great broken wings, while the giant waves dashed higher above the deck, washing many of the bodies overboard and wetting the little boy to the skin. Shivering with cold, he gave himself up for lost and prayed to the gods, whom his mother had often told him about, to take him from this dreadful ship and let him escape the fatal illness.

FAIRY HELPERS

As he lay there praying, he heard a slight noise in the rigging just above his head. Looking up, he saw a ball of fire running along a yardarm near the top of the mast. The sight was so strange that he forgot his prayer and stared with open-mouthed wonder. To his astonishment, the ball grew brighter and brighter, and then suddenly began slipping down the mast, all the time increasing in size. Nearer and nearer came the fireball. At last, when it reached the deck, to Ying-lo's surprise, something very, very strange happened. Before he had time to feel alarmed, the light vanished, and a funny little man stood in front of him peering anxiously into the child's frightened face.

"Yes, you are the lad I'm looking for," he said at last, speaking in a piping voice that almost made Ying-lo smile. "You are Ying-lo, and you are the only one left of this wretched company."

Although he saw that the old man meant him no harm, the child could say nothing, but waited in

silence, wondering what would happen next.

By this time the vessel was tossing and pitching so violently that it seemed every minute as if it would upset and go down beneath the foaming waves, never to rise again. Not many miles distant on the right, some jagged rocks stuck out of the water, lifting their cruel heads as if waiting for the helpless ship.

The newcomer walked slowly towards the mast and tapped on it three times with an iron staff he had been using as a cane. Immediately the sails spread, the vessel righted itself and began to glide over the sea so fast that the gulls were soon left far behind, while the threatening rocks upon which the ship had been so nearly dashed seemed like specks in the distance.

"Do you remember me?" said the stranger, turning and coming up to Ying-lo, but his voice was lost in the whistling of the wind, and the boy knew only by the moving of his lips that the old man was talking. The greybeard came close and whispered to Ying-lo, "Did you ever see me before?"

With a puzzled look, at first the child shook his head. Then as he gazed more closely there seemed to be something that he recognized about the wrinkled face. "Yes, I think so, but I don't know when."

With a tap of his staff the fairy stopped the blowing of the wind, and then spoke once more to his small companion, "One year ago I passed through your village. I was dressed in rags, and was begging my way along the street, trying to find someone who would feel sorry for me. Alas! No one answered my cry for mercy. Not a crust was thrown into my bowl. All the people were deaf, and fierce dogs drove me from door to door. I was almost dying of hunger when I began to feel that here was a village without one good person in it. Just then you saw my suffering, and brought me out food. Your heartless mother saw you doing this and beat you cruelly. Do you remember now, my child?"

"Yes, I remember," he answered sadly, "and my mother is now lying dead. All are dead, my father and my brothers also. Not one is left of my family."

"Little did you know, my boy, to whom you were giving food that day. You took me for a lowly beggar, but, behold, it was not a poor man that you fed, for I am Iron Staff. You must have heard of me when they were telling of the fairies in the Western Heaven, and of their adventures here on earth."

"Yes, yes," answered Ying-lo, trembling half with fear and half with joy, "indeed I have heard of you many, many times, and all the people love you for your kind deeds of mercy."

"Alas! They did not show their love, my little one. Surely you know that if any one wishes to reward the fairies for their mercies, he must begin to do deeds of the same kind himself. No one but you in all your village had pity on me in my rags."

Ying-lo listened in wonder to Iron Staff, and when he had finished, the boy's face was glowing with the love of which the fairy had spoken. "My poor, poor father and mother!" he cried, "they knew nothing of these beautiful things you are telling me. They were brought up in poverty. As they were knocked about in childhood by those around them, so they learned to beat others who begged them for help. Is it strange that they did not have hearts full of pity for you when you looked like a beggar?"

"But what about you, my boy? You were not deaf when I asked you. Have you not been whipped and punished all your life? How then did you learn to look with love at those in tears?"

The child could not answer, but looked sadly at Iron Staff. "Oh, can you not, good fairy, restore my parents and brothers, and give them another chance to be good and useful people?"

"Listen, Ying-lo, it is impossible unless you do two things first," he answered, stroking his beard gravely and leaning heavily upon his staff.

"What are they? What must I do to save my family? Anything you ask of me will not be too much to pay for your kindness."

"First you must tell me of some good deed done by these people for whose lives you are asking. Name only one, for that will be enough, but it is against the rules of the fairies to help those who have done nothing."

Ying-lo was silent, and for a moment his face was clouded. "Yes, I know," he answered, brightening. "Last year when the foreigner rode through our village and fell sick in front of our house, they cared for him."

"How long?" asked the other sharply.

"Until he died the next week."

"And what did they do with the mule he was riding, his bed, and the money in his bag? Did they try to restore them to his people?"

"No, they said they'd keep them to pay for the trouble." Ying-lo's face turned scarlet.

The Phantom Vessel

"But you should try again, dear boy! Is there not one little deed of goodness that was not selfish? Think once more."

For a long time Ying-lo did not reply. At length he spoke in a low voice, "I think of one, but I fear it amounts to nothing."

"No good, my child, is too small to be counted when the gods are weighing a man's heart."

"Last spring the birds were eating in my father's garden. My mother wanted to buy poison from the shop to destroy them, but my father said no, that the little things must live, and he for one was not in favour of killing them."

"At last, Ying-lo, you have named a real deed of mercy, and as he spared the tiny birds from poison, so shall his life and the lives of your mother and brothers be restored from the deadly plague.

"But remember there is one other thing that depends on you."

Ying-lo's eyes glistened gratefully. "Then if it rests with me, and I can do it, you have my promise."

"Very well, Ying-lo. What I require is that you carry out to the letter my instructions. Now it is time for me to keep my promise to you."

So saying, Iron Staff called on Ying-lo to point out the members of his family, and, approaching them one by one, with the end of his iron stick he touched their foreheads. In an instant each, without a word, arose. Looking round and recognizing Ying-lo, they stood back, frightened at seeing him with the fairy. Iron Staff beckoned all of them to listen. This they did willingly, too much terrified to speak, for they saw on all sides signs of the plague that had swept over the vessel, and they remembered the frightful agony they had suffered in dying. Each knew that he had been lifted by some magic power from darkness into light.

The Phantom Vessel

"My friends," began the fairy, "little did you think when less than a year ago you drove me from your door that soon you yourselves would be in need of mercy. As you look back through your wicked lives can you think of any reason why you deserved this rescue? No, there is no memory of goodness in your black hearts. Well, I shall tell you – it is this little boy, this Ying-lo, who many times has felt the weight of your wicked hands and has hidden in terror at your coming. To him alone you owe my help.

"If at any time you treat him badly and do not heed his wishes – mark you well my words – by the power of this magic staff which I shall place in his hands, he may enter at once into the land of the fairies, leaving you to die in your wickedness. This I command him to do, and he has promised to obey my slightest wish.

"This plague took you off suddenly and ended your wicked lives. Ying-lo has raised you from its grasp and his power can lift you from the bed of sin. No other hand than his can bear the rod which I am leaving. If one of you but touch it, instantly he will fall dead upon the ground.

"And now, my child, the time has come for me to leave you. First, however, I must show you what you are now able to do. Around you lie the corpses of sailors and passengers. Tap three times upon the mast and wish that they shall come to life." So saying he handed Ying-lo the iron staff.

Although the magic rod was heavy, the child lifted it as if it were a fairy's wand. Then, stepping forward to the mast, he rapped three times as he had been commanded. Immediately on all sides arose the bodies, once more full of life and strength.

"Now command the ship to take you back to your home port, for such sinful creatures as these are in no way fit to make a journey among strangers. They must first return and free their homes of sin."

Again rapping on the mast, the child willed the

194

great vessel to take its homeward course. No sooner
had he moved the staff than the boat swung round
and started on the return journey. Swifter than a
flash of lightning it flew, for it had become a fairy
vessel. Before the sailors and the travellers could
recover from their surprise, land was sighted and
they saw that they were entering the harbour.

Just as the ship was darting toward the shore the
fairy suddenly changed into a ball of fire which
rolled along the deck and ascended the spars. As it
reached the top of the rigging it floated off into the
sky, and all on board watched it until it vanished.

With a cry of thanksgiving, Ying-lo flung his
arms about his parents and descended with them to
the shore.

Farmer Mybrow
and the Fairies

By William H Barker

Farmer Mybrow was one day looking about for a suitable piece of land to convert into a field, for he wished to grow corn and yams. He discovered a fine spot, close to a great forest – which was the home of some fairies. He set to work at once to prepare the field.

Having sharpened his great knife, he began to cut down the bushes. No sooner had he touched one than he heard a voice say, "Who is there, cutting down the bushes?"

Mybrow was too much astonished to answer. The question was repeated. This time the farmer realized that it must be one of the fairies, and so replied, "I am Mybrow, come to prepare a field."

Fortunately for him the fairies were in great good humour. He heard one say, "Let us all help Farmer Mybrow to cut down the bushes." The rest agreed. To Mybrow's great delight, the bushes were all rapidly cut down with very little trouble on his part. He returned home, exceedingly well pleased with his day's work, having resolved to keep the field a secret even from his wife.

Early in January, when it was time to burn the dry bush, he set off to his field, one afternoon, with the means of making a fire. Hoping to have the fairies' help once more, he struck the trunk of a tree as he passed. Immediately came the question, "Who is there, striking the stumps?"

FAIRY HELPERS

He promptly replied, "I am Mybrow, come to burn down the bush." Accordingly, the dried bushes were all burned down, and the field left clear in less time that it takes to tell it.

Next day the same thing happened. Mybrow came to chop up the stumps for firewood and clear the field for digging. In a very short time his firewood was piled ready, while the field was bare.

So it went on. The field was divided into two parts – one for maize and one for yams. In all the preparations – digging, sowing, planting – the fairies gave great assistance. Still, the farmer had managed to keep the whereabouts of his field a secret from his wife and neighbours.

The soil having been so carefully prepared, the crops promised exceedingly well. Mybrow visited them from time to time, and congratulated himself on the splendid harvest he would have.

One day, while maize and yams were still in their green and milky state, Mybrow's wife came to him. She wished to know where his field lay, that she might go and fetch some of the firewood from it. At first he refused to tell her. Being very persistent, however, she finally succeeded in obtaining the information – but on one condition. She must not answer any question that should be asked her. This she readily promised, and set off for the field.

When she arrived there she was utterly amazed at the wealth of the corn and yams. She had never seen such magnificent crops. The maize looked most tempting – being still in the milky state – so she plucked an ear. While doing so she heard a voice say, "Who is there, breaking the corn?"

"Who dares ask me such a question?" she replied angrily, for she had quite forgotten her husband's command. Going to the field of yams she plucked one of them also.

"Who is there, picking the yams?" came the question again.

"It is I, Mybrow's wife. This is my husband's field and I have a right to pick." Out came the fairies.

"Let us all help Mybrow's wife to pluck her corn and yams," said they. And before the frightened woman could say a word, the fairies had all set to work with a will, and within a moment, all the corn and yams lay useless on the ground. They were not ready for picking, being all green and unripe, so the harvest was now utterly spoiled. The farmer's wife wept bitterly, but to no purpose. She returned slowly home, not knowing what to say to her husband about such a terrible catastrophe. She decided to keep silence about the matter.

Accordingly, next day the poor man set off gleefully to his field to see how his fine crops were going on. His anger and dismay may be imagined when he saw his field a complete ruin. All his work and foresight had been absolutely ruined through his wife's forgetfulness of her promise.

MAGIC AND MISCHIEF

The Fairy Cure

By Patrick Kennedy

For nearly a year, Nora's daughter, Judy, had been confined to her bed by a sore leg, which neither she nor the neighbouring doctor could 'make any hand of.'

Now Nora's mother was a midwife, and one night she was summoned by a dark rider to help with a lady about to have a child. She was whisked away and brought to the door of a magnificent palace. In the hall she was surprised to see an old neighbour, who had long been spirited away from the haunts of his youth and manhood. He at once took an opportunity, when the dark man was not observing him, to warn Nora that if she ever wanted to return home, she must take no refreshment of any kind while under the roof of the fairy castle, and refuse money or any other reward in any form. The only exception he made was in favour of cures for diseases inflicted by evil spirits or by fairies.

She found the lady of the castle in a bed with pillows and quilts of silk, and in a short time (for Nora was a handy woman) there was a beautiful little girl sleeping peacefully with the delighted mother. All the fine ladies that were scattered through the large room now gathered round, and congratulated their queen, and paid many compliments to the lucky-handed Nora. "I am so pleased with you," said the lady, "that I shall be glad to see you take as much gold, and silver, and jewels, out of the next room, as you can carry."

Nora stepped in out of curiosity and saw piles of gold and silver coins, and baskets of diamonds and pearls. Great heaps of treasure were lying about on every side, but she remembered her caution, and came out empty-handed.

"I'm much obliged to you, my lady," said she, "but if I took them guineas, and crowns, and jewels home, no one would ever call on me again to help his wife, and I'd be sitting and doing nothing but drinking tea, an' I'm sure I'd be dead before a year'd be gone by."

"Oh dear!" said the lady, "What an odd person you are! At any rate, sit down at that table, and help yourself to food and drink."

"Oh, ma'am, is it them jellies, an' custards, an' pastry you'd like to see me at? Lord love you! I would'n know the way to me mouth with the likes of them."

"Alas! Alas! Is there any way in which I can show

you how grateful I am for your help and your skill?"

"Indeed there is, ma'am. My girl, Jude, is lying under a sore leg for a twelvemonth, an' I'm sure that the lord or yourself can make her as sound as a bell if you only say the word."

"Ask me anything but that, and I shall see that you have it."

"Oh, lady, dear, that's giving me everything but the thing I want."

"You don't know the offence your daughter gave to us, I am sure, or you would not have asked me to cure her."

"Judy offend you, ma'am! Oh, it's impossible!"

"Not at all, and this is the way it happened. You know that all the fairy court enjoy their lives in the night only, and we frequently go through the country, and hold our feasts where the kitchen, and especially the hearth, is swept up clean. About a twelvemonth ago, myself and my ladies were passing your cabin, and one of the company liked the appearance of the neat thatch, and the whitewashed walls, and the clean pavement outside the door, so much, that she persuaded us all to go in. We found the cheerful fire shining, the well swept hearth and floor, and the clean pewter and beautiful plates on the dresser, and the white table. We were so well pleased, that we sat down on the hearth, and laid our tea tray, and began to drink our tea as comfortably as could be. You know we can be any size we please, and there was a score of us settled before the fire.

"We were vexed enough when we saw your daughter come up out of your bedroom, and make towards the fire. Her feet, I acknowledge, were white and clean, but one of them would cover two or three of us, the size we were that night. On she came stalking, and just as I was raising my cup of tea to my lips, down came the soft flat sole on it, and spilled the tea all over me. I was very much annoyed, and I caught the thing that came next to

my hand, and hurled it at her.
It was the teapot, and the point
of the spout is in her leg from that
night till now."

"Oh, lady! How can you hold spite to
the poor girl, that knew no more of you
being there, nor of offending you, that
she did of the night she was born?"

"Well, well, now that is all past
and gone. Take this ointment.
Rub it where you will see the
purple mark, and I hope that
your future thoughts of me
may be pleasant."

Just then, a messenger
came to say that the lord was at the
hall door waiting for Nora, for the
cockerels would be soon crowing. So she
took leave of the lady, and mounted behind the
dark man. The horse's back seemed as hard and as

thin as a hazel stick, but it bore her safely to her home. She was in a sleepy state all the time she was returning, but at last she woke up, and found herself standing by her own door. She got into bed as fast as she could, and when she woke next morning, she fancied it was all a dream. But she put her hand in her pocket, and there, for a certainty, was the box of ointment. She went to her daughter's room and without waking her, rubbed some of the stuff on her leg. In a few seconds she saw the skin bursting, and a tiny spout of a teapot working itself out.

When Judy awoke she wondered at the ease she felt in her leg. She rejoiced at her mother's story and soon regained her strength. From then on she always left the kitchen spotless at night, and took care never to let her feet stray after bedtime, for fear of giving offence to unseen visitors.

A French Puck

By Paul Sébillot

*A*mong the mountain pastures and valleys that lie in the centre of France there dwelt a mischievous kind of spirit (whom we will call Puck), whose delight it was to play tricks on everybody, and particularly on the shepherds. They never knew when they were safe from him, as he could change himself into a man, woman or child, a stick, a goat or a ploughshare. Indeed, there was only one thing whose shape he could not take, and that was a needle. At least, he could transform himself into a needle, but he never was able to imitate the hole, so every woman would have found him out at once, and this he knew.

Puck was careful not always to play his tricks in the same place, but always moved on from one village to another, so that everyone trembled lest he should be the next victim.

One day he was told of a young couple who were going to the nearest town to buy all that they needed for setting up house. Quite certain that they would forget something which they could not do without, Puck waited patiently till they were jogging along in their cart on their return journey, and changed himself into a fly in order to overhear their conversation. For a long time it was very dull – all about their wedding day next month, and who would be invited. This led the bride to her dress, and she gave a cry of dismay.

A French Puck

"Oh how could I be so stupid? I have forgotten to buy the coloured reels of cotton to match my clothes!"

"Dear, dear!" exclaimed the young man. "That is unlucky, and didn't you tell me that the dressmaker was coming in tomorrow?"

"Yes, I did," and then she gave another little cry, which had quite a different sound from the first, and said, "Look!"

The bridegroom looked, and on one side of the road he saw a large ball of thread of all colours – of all the colours, that is, of the dresses that were tied on to the back of the cart.

"Well, that is a wonderful piece of good fortune," cried he, as he sprang out of the cart to get it. "One would think a fairy had put it there on purpose."

"Perhaps she has," laughed the girl, and as she spoke she seemed to hear an echo of her laughter.

For a moment she thought it was coming from the horse, but of course that was nonsense.

The dressmaker was delighted with the thread that was given her. It matched the clothes so perfectly, and never tied itself in knots, or broke perpetually, as most thread did. She finished her work much quicker than she expected and the bride invited her to come to the church and see her in her wedding dress.

There was a great crowd assembled to witness the ceremony, for the young people were immense favourites in the neighbourhood, and their parents were very rich. The doors were open, and the beautiful bride could be seen from afar, walking under the chestnut avenue.

"What a beautiful girl!" exclaimed the men. "What a lovely dress!" whispered the women. But just as she entered the church and took the hand of the bridegroom, who was waiting for her, a loud noise was heard – *Crick! Crack! Crick! Crack!* – and the wedding garments fell to the ground, to the great confusion of the wearer.

Not that the ceremony was put off for a little thing like that! Cloaks were instantly offered to the young bride, but she was so upset that she could hardly keep from tears.

One of the guests, more curious than the rest, stayed behind to examine the dress, to find out the cause of the disaster. "The thread must have been rotten," she said to herself. "I will see if I can break it." But search as she would she could find none. The thread had vanished!

The Fairy
Fluffikins

By Michael Fairless

The Fairy Fluffikins lived in a warm woolly nest
in a hole down an old oak tree. She was the
sweetest, funniest little fairy you ever saw. She wore
a little, soft dress, and on her head a little woolly cap.
Fairy Fluffikins had red hair and the brightest,
naughtiest, sharpest brown eyes imaginable.

What a life she led the animals! Fairy Fluffikins
was a sad tease. She would creep into the nests

where the fat baby dormice were asleep in bed while mamma dormouse nodded over her knitting and papa smoked his little acorn pipe, and she would tickle the babies till they screamed with laughter.

One night she had fine fun. She found a little dead mouse in a field, and an idea struck her. She hunted about till she found a piece of long, strong grass, and then she took the little mouse, tied the piece of grass round its tail, and ran away with it to the big tree where the ancient owl lived. There was a little hole at the bottom of the tree and into it Fairy Fluffikins crept, leaving the mouse outside in the moonlight. Presently she heard a gruff voice in the tree saying, "I smell mouse, I smell mouse." Then there was a swoop of wings, and Fairy Fluffikins promptly drew the mouse into the little hole and stuffed its tail into her mouth so that she might not be heard laughing, and the gruff voice said angrily, "Where's that mouse gone? I smelt mouse, I know I smelt mouse!"

She grew tired of this game after a few times, so she left the mouse in the hole and crept away to a new one. She really was a very naughty fairy. She blew on the buttercups so that they thought the morning breeze had come to wake them up, and opened their cups in a great hurry. She buzzed outside the clover and made it talk in its sleep, so that it said in a cross, sleepy voice, "Go away, you stupid busy bee, and don't wake me up in the middle of the night."

She pulled the tail of the nightingale who was singing to his lady love in the hawthorn bush, and he lost his place in his song.

Next she took to tormenting the squirrels. She used to find their stores of nuts and carry them away and fill the holes with pebbles, and this, when you are a hard-working squirrel with a large family to support, is very trying to the temper. Then she would tie acorns to their tails, and she would clap her hands to frighten them, and pull the baby

The Fairy Fluffikins

squirrels' ears, till at last they offered a reward to anyone who could catch Fairy Fluffikins and bring her to be punished.

No one caught Fairy Fluffikins – but she caught herself, as you shall hear.

She was poking about round a haystack one night, trying to find something naughty to do, when she came upon a sweet little house with pretty wire walls and a wooden door standing invitingly open. In hopped Fluffikins, thinking she was going to have some new kind of fun. There was a little white thing dangling from the roof, and she laid hold of it. Immediately there was a bang, the wooden door slammed, and Fluffikins was caught.

How she cried and stamped and pushed at the door, and promised to be a good fairy and a great many other things! But all to no purpose, the door was tight shut, and Fluffikins was not like some fortunate fairies who can get out of anywhere.

There she had to remain, and in the morning one

of the labourers found her, and, thinking she was some kind of dormouse, he carried her home to his little girl, and if you call on Mary Ann Smith you will see Fairy Fluffikins there still in a little cage. There is no one to tease and no mischief to get into, so if there is a miserable little fairy anywhere it is Fairy Fluffikins, and I'm not sure it doesn't serve her quite right.

Iktomi and the Ducks

By Zitkala-sa

*I*ktomi is a spider fairy. He wears brown deerskin leggings with long soft fringes on either side, and tiny beaded moccasins on his feet. His long black hair is parted in the middle and wrapped with red, red bands. He even paints his funny face with red and yellow, and draws big black rings around his eyes. He wears a beautifully warm deerskin jacket, with bright coloured beads sewed tightly on it.

Iktomi and the Ducks

Indeed, Iktomi dresses like a real Dakota brave.

Iktomi is a wily fellow. He prefers to spread a snare rather than to earn the smallest thing with honest hunting. Why, he laughs outright with wide open mouth when some simple folk are caught in a trap, sure and fast.

Thus Iktomi lives alone in a cone-shaped wigwam upon the plain. One day he sat hungry within his teepee. Suddenly he rushed out, dragging his blanket after him. Quickly spreading it on the ground, he tore up dry tall grass with both his hands and tossed it fast into the blanket.

Tying all the four corners together in a knot, he threw the light bundle of grass over his shoulder.

Snatching up a slender willow stick with his free left hand, he started off with a leap. Soon he came to the edge of the great level land. On the hilltop he paused for breath. With a thin palm shading his eyes from the western sun, he peered far away into the lowlands.

"Ah ha!" grunted he, satisfied with what he saw.

A group of wild ducks were dancing and feasting in the marshes. With wings outspread, tip to tip, they moved up and down in a large circle. Within the ring, around a small drum, sat the chosen singers, nodding their heads and blinking their eyes. They sang in unison a merry dance-song, and beat a lively tattoo on the drum.

Following a winding footpath soon came along the bent figure of a Dakota brave. He bore on his back a very large bundle. With a willow cane he propped himself up as he staggered along beneath his burden.

"Ho! Who is there?" called out a curious old duck, still bobbing up and down in the strange circular dance.

"Ho, Iktomi! Old fellow, pray tell us what you carry in your blanket. Do not hurry off! Stop! Halt!" urged one of the singers.

"My friends, I must not spoil your dance. Oh,

you would not care to see if you only knew what is in my blanket. Sing on! Dance on! I must not show you what I carry on my back," answered Iktomi. Now all the ducks crowded about Iktomi.

"We must see what you carry! We must know what is in your blanket!" they shouted in both his ears. Some even brushed their wings against the mysterious bundle.

Wily Iktomi replied, "My friends, it is only a pack of songs I carry in my blanket."

"Oh, then let us hear your songs!" cried the curious ducks.

At length Iktomi consented to sing his songs, and with great delight all the ducks flapped their wings and cried together, "Hoye! Hoye!"

Iktomi, with great care, laid down his bundle on the ground.

"I will build first a round straw house, for I never sing my songs in the open air," said he.

Quickly he bent green willow sticks, planting

both ends of each pole into the earth. These he covered thick with reeds and grasses. Soon the straw hut was ready. One by one the fat ducks waddled in through a small opening, which was the only entrance way.

In a strange low voice Iktomi began to sing his queer old tunes. All the ducks sat round-eyed in a circle about the mysterious singer. It was very dim inside the straw hut. All of a sudden his song burst into full voice. These were the words he sang:

Istokmus wacipo, tuwayatunwanpi kinhan ista nisasapi kta.

This means, 'With eyes closed you must dance. He who dares to open his eyes, forever red eyes shall have.'

Up rose the circle of seated ducks and holding their wings close against their sides began to dance to the rhythm of Iktomi's song and drum.

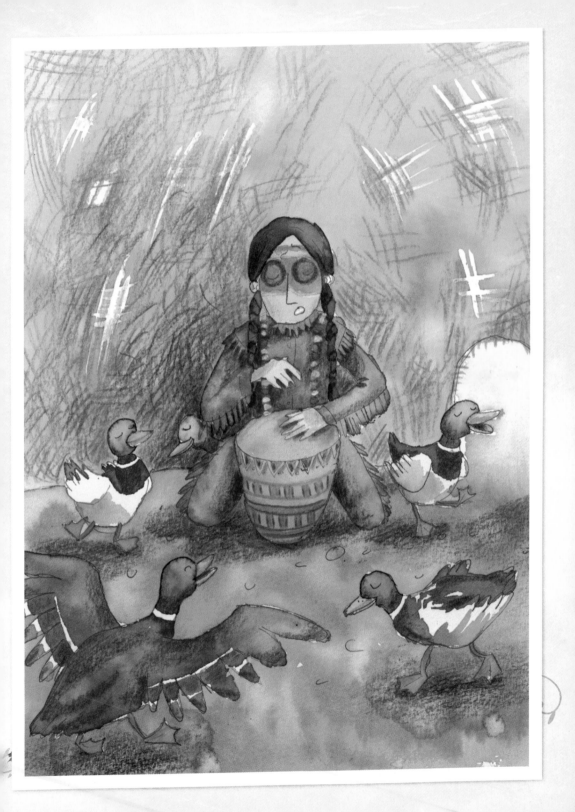

With eyes closed they did dance! Iktomi ceased to beat his drum. He began to sing louder and faster. He seemed to be moving about in the centre of the ring. No duck dared blink a wink. Each one shut his eyes very tight and danced even harder.

At length one of the dancers could close his eyes no longer! It was a Skiska who peeped the least tiny blink at Iktomi within the centre of the circle.

"Oh! Oh!" squawked he in awful terror, "Run! Fly! Iktomi is twisting your heads and breaking your necks! Run out and fly! Fly!" he cried.

Hereupon the ducks opened their eyes. There beside Iktomi's bundle of songs lay half of their crowd – flat on their backs.

Out they flew through the opening Skiska had made as he rushed forth with his alarm.

But as they soared high into the blue sky they cried to one another, "Oh! Your eyes are red-red!"

"And yours are red-red!" For the warning words had proven true.

Iktomi and the Ducks

"Ah ha!" laughed Iktomi, untying the four corners of his blanket, "I shall sit no more hungry within my dwelling."

Homewards he trudged along with nice fat ducks in his blanket. He left the little straw hut for the rains and winds to pull down.

The Fairies and the Envious Neighbour

By Algernon Freeman-Mitford

Once upon a time there was a man, who, being overtaken by darkness among the mountains, was driven to seek shelter in the trunk of a hollow tree. In the middle of the night, a group of fairies assembled at the place. The man, peeping out from his hiding place, was frightened out of his wits. But after a while the fairies began to feast and drink wine, and to amuse themselves by singing and

The Fairies and the Envious Neighbour

dancing, until at last the man forgot all about his fright, and crept out of his hollow tree to join in the revels.

When the day was about to dawn, the fairies said to the man, "You're a jolly companion, and must come out and dance with us again. You must promise." Thinking to bind him to return, the fairies took a large wart that grew on the man's forehead and kept it as a pledge.

The man walked home, gleeful that he had passed a jovial night, and got rid of his wart into the bargain. He told the story to all his friends, who congratulated him warmly on being cured of his wart.

But he had a neighbour who was also troubled with a wart of long standing. Envious of his friend's luck, this man went to find the hollow tree, in which he passed the night.

Towards midnight the elves came, as expected, and began to feast and drink and sing and dance as before. As soon as he saw this, he came out of his hollow tree, and began dancing and singing as his neighbour had done. The elves, mistaking him for their former companion, were delighted to see him, and said, "You're a good fellow to recollect your promise, and we'll give you back your pledge."

So one of the elves pulled the pawned wart out of his pocket and stuck it onto the man's forehead, on top of the wart he already had.

The envious neighbour went home weeping, with two warts instead of one. This is a good lesson to people who cannot see the good luck of others without coveting it for themselves.

Drak, the Fairy

By Kate Douglas Wiggin

*I*n the last century there lived in the little town of Gaillac, in Languedoc, a young merchant named Michael, who, having arrived at an age when he wished to settle down in life, sought a wife. Providing she was sweet-tempered, witty, rich, beautiful, and of good family, he was not particular about the rest. Unhappily, he could not see in Gaillac one who appeared worthy of his choice. At length he was told of a young lady in Lavaur with good qualities and a dowry of twenty thousand crowns. This sum was exactly that required by Michael to establish himself in business, so he instantly fell in love with the young lady of Lavaur. He obtained an introduction to the family, who liked his appearance, and gave him a good reception. But the young heiress had many suitors, from whom she hesitated to make a definite choice. After several discussions it was decided by her parents that the suitors should be brought together at a ball, and after having compared them a choice should be made.

On the appointed day Michael set out for Lavaur. His case was packed with his finest clothes – an apple-green coat, a lavender waistcoat, breeches of black velvet, silk stockings with silver trees, buckled shoes, powder box to powder his hair, and a satin ribbon for his pigtail. His horse was harnessed with gay trappings.

Drak, the Fairy

Furthermore, the prudent traveller, not having a pistol to put in his holsters, had slipped in a little bottle of wine and several slices of almond cake, in order to have something at hand to keep his courage up. For in reality, now that the day had come he was in a very anxious state, and when he saw in the distance the church of Lavaur he felt quite taken aback. He slackened the pace of his horse, then dismounted, and in order to reflect upon what he should do at the ball he entered a little wood and sat down on the turf. He drew from his holsters, to keep him company, the almond cake and the bottle. The latter he placed between his knees, so that without thinking of it he varied his reflections by sips of wine and mouthfuls of cake.

The sun having disappeared from the horizon he was about to pursue his journey, when he heard a sound behind him among the leaves, as of a multitude of little footsteps trampling the grass in tune to the music of a flute and cymbals.

Astonished, he turned around, and by the light of the first stars, he perceived a troop of fairies, who were running, headed by the king, Tambourinet. In their rear, turning over and over like a wheel, was the buffoon of the little people – Drak, the fairy.

The fairies surrounded the traveller, and gave him a thousand welcomes and good wishes. Michael, who had drunk too freely not to be brave, began to crumble and throw his cake to them as one would to the birds. Each one had his crumb with the exception of Drak, who arrived when everyone had finished. King Tambourinet next asked what was in the bottle, and the fairies passed it from hand to hand till it reached the buffoon, who, finding it empty, threw it away.

Michael burst out laughing. "That is justice, my little man," said he to the fairy. "For those who arrive late, there remains nothing but regret."

"I will make you remember what you have just said," cried Drak in anger.

Drak, the Fairy

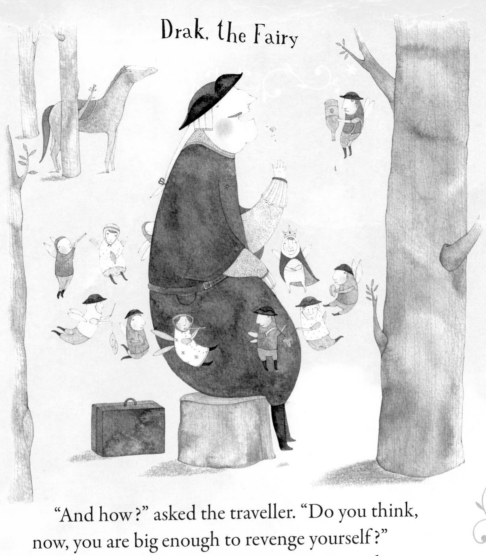

"And how?" asked the traveller. "Do you think, now, you are big enough to revenge yourself?"

Drak disappeared without answering, and Michael, after taking leave of Tambourinet, mounted his horse.

He had not gone a hundred paces, when the

saddle turned and threw him roughly to the ground. He arose a little stunned, rebuckled the straps, and mounted again. A little farther on, as he was going over a bridge, the right stirrup bent slightly, and he found himself thrown in the middle of the river. He got out again in a very bad humour, and fell the third time over the pebbles in the road, hurting himself so much that he could hardly proceed. He began to think that if he persisted in riding in the saddle he would be unable to present himself at all to the family of the young lady, so he decided to ride his horse barebacked, and take the saddle upon his shoulder. In this manner, he made his entry into Lavaur amid the laughter of the people who were sitting at their doors.

At length he reached the inn, where he alighted, and asked for a room in which to change his travelling clothes. Having obtained a chamber, he proceeded with much care to open his suitcase and lay out carefully on the bed the articles he needed.

Drak, the Fairy

His first consideration was whether he should powder his hair white or yellow. Having decided it should be white, he seized his swans-down powder puff, and commenced the operation on the right side. But the moment he had finished that side he saw that an invisible hand had powdered the other side yellow, so that his head had the appearance of a half-peeled lemon. Michael, stupefied, stretched out his hand toward the reel on which the ribbon for his pigtail was wound. The reel escaped from his fingers and fell to the ground.

Michael went to pick it up, but it seemed to roll before him. Twenty times he was about to seize it, and twenty times his impatient hands missed it. One would have said he looked like a kitten playing with a reel. At length, seeing that time was going, he lost patience and resigned himself to wearing his old ribbon.

He now hastened to put on his morocco shoes. He buckled the right, then having finished the left, he stopped to admire them, but as he did so the right buckle fell to the ground. He replaced it, but no sooner had he done so than the left followed suit. Furious, he finished by putting on his travelling boots, and was about to put on his velvet breeches, when, immediately he approached the bed, the breeches began of their own accord to walk about the room.

Michael, petrified, stood mute, with his arm extended, watching this incongruous dance. But you may guess how he looked when he saw the vest, coat and hat join the breeches and form a sort of counterfeit of himself, which commenced to walk about and copy his movements.

Pale with fear Michael drew back to the window, but at this moment the peculiar figure turned towards him, and he saw, peering from beneath the brim of his own cocked hat, the mischevious face of Drak, the fairy.

Michael uttered a cry. "It is you, you villain, is it?

Drak, the Fairy

I'll make you repent of your insolence if you don't instantly give me back my clothes."

So saying, he rushed to take them, but the fairy, turning sharply around, ran to the other side of the room. Michael was beside himself with anger and impatience, and rushed again towards the fairy, who this time passed between his legs and rushed out on

to the staircase. Michael pursued him angrily up
four flights of stairs till they arrived at the garret,
where the fairy dodged round and round, and then
skipped out of the window. Michael, exasperated,
took the same route. The malicious fairy led him
from roof to roof, dragging the velvet breeches, the
vest, and coat in all the gutters, to Michael's despair.

The young gallant sat down upon the roof with a
cry of despair, but rising immediately, said with
resolution, "Well then, I'll go to the ball in my
travelling dress."

"Hark!" interrupted the fairy.

The sound of a bell rang out from a neighbouring
steeple. Midnight struck! Michael counted the
twelve strokes, and could not restrain a cry. It was
the hour designated by the parents when they
would proclaim their daughter's choice for a
husband. He wrung his hands in despair.

"Unhappy man that I am!" Michael cried. "By
the time I arrive all will be over, and she and her

parents will laugh at me."

"And that would be justice, my big man," replied Drak. "For you have said yourself, 'For those who arrive late, there remains nothing but regret.' This time will serve you, I hope, as a lesson and prevent you another time from laughing at the feeble, for from henceforth you will know that the smallest are big enough to avenge themselves."

Iktomi and the Muskrat

By Zitkala-sa

*B*eside a white lake, beneath a large grown willow tree, sat Iktomi the fairy on the bare ground. With ankles crossed together around a pot of soup, Iktomi bent over some delicious boiled fish.

Fast he dipped his black horn spoon into the soup, for he was ravenous. Iktomi had no regular meal times. Often when he was hungry he went without food.

Iktomi and the Muskrat

"How, how, my friend!" said a voice out of the wild rice.

Iktomi started. He almost choked on his soup. He peered through the long reeds from where he sat with his long horn spoon in mid-air.

"How, my friend!" said the voice again, this time close at his side. Iktomi turned and there stood a dripping muskrat who had just come out of the lake.

"Oh, it is my friend who startled me. I wondered if among the wild rice some spirit voice was talking. How, how, my friend!" said Iktomi. The muskrat stood smiling. On his lips hung a ready 'Yes, my friend,' for when Iktomi would ask, 'My friend, will you sit down beside me and share my food?'

That was the custom of the plains people. Yet Iktomi sat silent. He hummed an old song and beat gently on the pot with his buffalo-horn spoon. The muskrat began to feel awkward before such lack of hospitality and wished himself under water.

After many heart throbs Iktomi stopped drumming with his spoon, and looking upward into the muskrat's face, he said, "My friend, let us race to see who shall win this pot of fish. If I win, I shall not need to share it with you. If you win, you shall have half of it." Springing to his feet, Iktomi began at once to tighten the belt about his waist.

"My friend Iktomi, I cannot run a race with you! I am not a swift runner, and you are nimble as a deer," answered the hungry muskrat.

For a moment Iktomi stood with a hand on his long protruding chin. The muskrat looked out of the corners of his eyes without moving his head. He watched the wily Iktomi concocting a plot.

"I shall carry a large stone on my back. That will slacken my usual speed, and the race will be a fair one."

Saying this he laid a firm hand upon the muskrat's shoulder and started off along the edge of the lake. When they reached the opposite side

Iktomi and the Muskrat

Iktomi pried about in search of a heavy stone.

At last he found one half-buried in the shallow water. Pulling it out upon dry land, he wrapped it in his blanket.

"Now, my friend, you shall run on the left side of the lake, I on the other. The race is for the boiled fish in yonder kettle!" said Iktomi.

The muskrat helped to lift the heavy stone upon Iktomi's back. Then they parted. Each took a narrow path through the tall reeds fringing the shore. Iktomi found his load a heavy one. Perspiration hung like beads on his brow. His chest heaved hard and fast.

He looked across the lake to see how far the muskrat had gone, but nowhere did he see any sign of him.

"Well, he is running low under the wild rice!" said he. Yet as he scanned the tall grasses on the lake shore, he saw not one stir as if to make way for the runner. "Ah, has he gone so fast ahead that the disturbed grasses in his trail have quieted again?" exclaimed Iktomi. With that thought he quickly dropped the heavy stone. "No more of this!" said he, patting his chest with both hands.

Off with a springing bound, he ran swiftly towards the goal. Tufts of reeds and grass fell flat under his feet. Hardly had they raised

Iktomi and the Muskrat

their heads when Iktomi was many paces gone.

Soon he reached the heap of cold ashes. Iktomi halted stiff as if he had struck an invisible cliff. His black eyes showed a ring of white about them as he stared at the empty ground. There was no pot of boiled fish! There was no muskrat in sight!

"Oh, if only I had shared my food like a real Dakota, I would not have lost it all! Why did I not remember the muskrat would run through the water? He swims faster than I could ever run! That is what he has done. He has laughed at me for carrying a weight on my back while he shot hither like an arrow!"

"Ha! Ha! Ha!" laughed the muskrat. "Next time, say to a visiting friend, 'Be seated beside me, my friend. Let me share my food with you.'"

VISITORS TO FAIRYLAND

A Boy that Visited Fairyland

By William Elliot Griffis

Many are the places in Wales where the ground is lumpy with burial mounds. Among these sheep graze, donkeys bray, and cows chew the cud.

Here the ground is strewn with the ruins of Welsh strongholds, of old Roman camps, and of chapels and monasteries, showing that many different races of men have come and gone, while the birds still fly and the flowers bloom.

Centuries ago, the monks of St David had a
school where lads were taught Latin and good
manners. One of their pupils was a boy named
Elidyr. He was such a poor scholar and he so hated
books and loved play, that in his case punishments
were almost of daily occurrence. One day, though
he was only twelve years old, the boy started on a
long run into the country. The further he got, the
happier he felt – at least for one day.

At night, tired out, he crept into a cave. When he
woke up in the morning, he thought it was glorious
to be as free as the wild asses. Like them, he quenched
his thirst at the brook. But by noon he had found
nothing to eat. His stomach seemed to enlarge with
very emptiness, and his hunger grew every minute.

He dared not go out far and pick berries, for he
saw that people were now out searching for him. He
did not feel like going back to books, rods and
scoldings, but the day seemed as long as a week and

he was glad when darkness came. His bed was no softer in the cave. At dawn, the question in his mind was still whether to stay and starve, or to go home and get two thrashings – one from his father, and another from the monks. Finally, he came to a stern resolve. He set out, ready to face two whippings, rather than one death by starvation.

But he did not have to go home yet, for at the cave's mouth, he met two elves, who delivered a most welcome message. "Come with us to a land full of fun, play, and good things to eat."

All at once, his hunger left him. All desire to go home, or to risk either schooling or a thrashing, passed away also.

Into a dark passage all three went, but they soon came out into a beautiful country, where birds sang and flowers bloomed! All around could be heard the shouts of little folks at play. Never did things look so lovely.

Soon, in front of the broad path along which

they were travelling, there rose up before him a glorious palace. It had a splendid gateway, and the silver-topped towers seemed to touch the blue sky.

"What is this place?" asked the lad of his guides. They made answer that it was the palace of the king of Fairyland. Then they led him into the throne room, where sat in golden splendour, a king of tiny stature but majestic presence, who was clad in resplendent robes. He was surrounded by courtiers in rich apparel, and all about him was magnificence, such as the boy Elidyr had neither read about before nor even dreamed.

Yet everything was so small that it looked like Toy Land, and he felt like a giant among them, even though many of the little men around him were old enough to have whiskers on their cheeks and beards on their chins.

The king spoke kindly to Elidyr, asking him who he was, and whence he had come.

While they were talking the prince, the king's only son, appeared. He was dressed in white velvet and gold, and had a long feather in his cap. In the pleasantest way, he took Elidyr's hand and said, "Glad to see you. Come and let us play together."

That was just what Elidyr liked to hear. They played with golden balls, and rode little horses with silver saddles and bridles, but these pretty animals were no larger than small dogs, or greyhounds.

No meat was ever seen on the table, but plenty of

milk. They never told a lie, nor used bad language. They often talked about mortal men, but usually to despise them. To the elves, human beings were never satisfied, or long happy, even when they got what they wanted.

Everything in this part of Fairyland was lovely, but it was always cloudy. No sun, star or moon was ever seen, yet the little men did not seem to mind it and enjoyed themselves every day. There was no end of play, and that suited Elidyr.

Yet by and by, he got tired even of games and play, and grew very homesick. He wanted to see his mother. So he asked the king to let him visit his old home. He promised solemnly to come back after a few hours. His majesty gave his permission, but charged him not to take with him anything whatever from Fairyland, and to go with only the clothes on his back.

The same two elves who had brought him into Fairyland were chosen to conduct him back. When they had led him again through the underground passage into the sunlight, they made him invisible until he arrived at his mother's cottage.

She was overjoyed to find that no wolf had torn him to pieces, or wild bull had pushed him over a steep cliff. She asked him many questions, and he told her all he had seen, felt, or known.

When he rose up to go, she begged him to stay longer, but he said he must keep his word. So he made his mother agree not to tell – not even to his father – as to where he was, or what he was doing. Then he made off and reported again to his playmates in Fairyland.

The king was pleased at the lad's promptness in returning. As a reward for keeping his word so faithfully and telling the truth, he allowed Elidyr to go and see his mother as often as he wanted to do so. He even gave orders releasing the two little men from constantly guarding him and told them to let the lad go alone, and whenever he liked, for he always kept his word – unlike other humans.

Many times did Elidyr visit his mother, and she loved to hear of his adventures in Fairyland. One day he spoke to her of the heavy yellow balls, with which he and the king's sons played, and how these rolled around.

Before leaving home, this boy had never seen gold, and did not know what it was, but his mother guessed that the yellow balls were made of the precious metal. So she begged him to bring one of them back to her.

This, Elidyr thought, would not be right, but after much argument, his parents being poor, and she telling him that out of hundreds in the king's palace, one single ball would not be missed, he decided to please her.

So one day he did not follow the princes to the throne room after play time. Instead Elidyr waited until he was alone, and then picked up one of the yellow balls and started off homeward.

But no sooner was he back on the earth, and in
the sunlight again, than he heard footsteps behind
him. Then he knew that he had been discovered.

He glanced over his shoulder and there were the
two little men, who had formerly been his guards.
They scowled at him as if they were mad enough to
bite off the heads of nails. Then they rushed after
him, and there began a race to the cottage.

A Boy that Visited Fairyland

But the boy had legs that were at least twice as long as the little men, and though they ran surprisingly fast he still managed to reach the cottage door first. He now thought himself safe, but pushing open the door, he stumbled over the copper threshold, and the ball rolled out of his hand, across the floor of hardened clay, almost reaching the white-washed border which ran about the edges of the room. It stopped at the feet of his mother, whose eyes opened wide at the sight of the ball of shining gold.

As poor Elidyr lay sprawling on the floor, and before he could pick himself up, one of the little guardsmen leaped over him, rushed into the room, and, from under his mother's petticoats, picked up the ball.

The two fairies spat at the boy and shouted, 'traitor', 'rascal', 'thief', 'false mortal', 'fox', 'rat', 'wolf', and other bad names. Then they turned on their heels and sped out of the door and away, one of them holding the precious gold ball tightly.

Now Elidyr, though he had been a mischievous boy, often wilful, lazy, and never studying his books, had always loved the truth. He was very sad because he had broken his word of honour to his fairy friends. So, almost mad with grief and shame, and from an accusing conscience, he went back to find the cave in which he had slept on the night he had run away. He knew in his heart that he should return to the king of the fairies, and ask his pardon, even if his majesty never allowed him to visit Fairyland again.

But though he returned often to that same place, and even spent whole days in searching those wild lands, he could never again discover the magical opening in the hills.

So, fully penitent, and resolving to live right, and become what his father wanted him to be, he went back to the monastery. There he plied his tasks so diligently that he excelled in all learning.

In time, he became one of the most famous scholars in Welsh history. When he died, he asked to be buried, not in the monk's cemetery, but with his father and mother, in the humble village churchyard. He had made a special request that no name, record, or epitaph be chiselled on his tomb, but only these words:

WE CAN DO NOTHING AGAINST THE TRUTH,
BUT ONLY FOR THE TRUTH.

The Fairy Wife

By Patrick Kennedy

This is one of the many stories in which a person is stolen away by the fairies, and another person hopes to rescue them, which usually takes great courage and steadfastness. In fairy stories from Ireland (where this tale is set), people who neglect their prayers or don't go to church are always at more risk of being stolen by the fairies. In this story, 'fairy man' means a man who claims to have skill in curing the illnesses and disorders that fairies cause.

There was once a little farmer and his wife living near Coolgarrow. They had three children, and my story happened while the youngest was a baby. The wife was a good woman, but her mind was always on her family and her farm. She worked so hard that she hardly ever had time to pray before falling asleep, and she thought the time spent in the chapel was twice as long as it need be. So one day, she let her husband and her two children go ahead of her to Mass, while she called to consult a fairy man about a disorder one of her cows had. She was late at the chapel, and was sorry all the day after, for her husband was in grief about it.

Late one night the farmer was wakened up by the cries of his children calling out, "Mother! Mother!"

When he sat up and rubbed his eyes, he found there was no wife by his side, and he asked the little ones what had become of their mother. They answered that they had seen the room full of nice little men and women, all dressed in clothes of white and red and green, and their mother in the middle of them, going out by the door as if she was walking in her sleep.

The farmer leapt out of bed, and searched

The Fairy Wife

everywhere round the house and down the road, but neither tale nor tidings did he get of her for many a day.

Well, the poor man was miserable enough, for he was as fond of his wife as she was of him. It used to bring the salt tears down his cheeks to see his poor children neglected and dirty, as they often were, and they would have been in an even worse state if it hadn't been for a kind neighbour that used to look in whenever she could spare time.

About six weeks after – just as the farmer was going out to his work one morning – a neighbour that used to mind women when they were ill came up to him, and kept step by step with him to the field. On the way, she told him, "Just as I was falling asleep last night, I heard a horse's tramp on the grass and a knock at the door, and there, when I came out, was a fine-looking dark man, mounted on a black horse. He told me to get ready in all haste, for a lady was in great want of me.

"As soon as I put on my cloak and things, he took me by the hand, and before I knew it I was sitting behind him. 'Where are we going, sir?' said I.

"'You'll soon know,' said he, and he drew his

fingers across my eyes, and not a ray could I see.

"I kept a tight grip of him, and I little knew whether we were going backwards or forwards, or how long we were about it, till my hand was taken again, and I felt the ground under me. The fingers went the other way across my eyes, and there we were before a castle door, and in we went through a big hall and great rooms all painted in fine green colours, with red and gold bands and ornaments, and the finest carpets and chairs and tables and window curtains, and beautiful ladies and grand gentlemen walking about.

"At last we came to a bedroom, with a beautiful lady in bed, with a fine bouncing boy beside her. The lady clapped her hands, and in came the dark man and kissed her and the baby, and praised me, and gave me a bottle of green ointment to rub the child all over.

"Well, the child I rubbed, sure enough, but my right eye began to smart, and I put up my finger and gave it a rub. And then I stared, for never in all my life was I so frightened. The beautiful room was really a big, rough cave, with water oozing over the edges of the stones and through the clay, and the

lady, and the lord, and the child were weazened,
poverty-bitten creatures – nothing but skin and
bone – and the rich dresses had turned to old rags.
I didn't let on that I found any difference, and after
a bit the dark man said, 'Go before me to the hall
door, and I will be with you in a few moments, and
see you safe home.'

"Well, just as I turned into the outside cave, who
should I see watching near the door but your poor
wife Molly. She looked round all terrified, and said
to me in a whisper, 'I'm brought here to nurse the
child of the king and queen of the fairies, but there
is one chance of saving me. All the court will pass
the cross near Templeshambo next Friday night, on
a visit to the fairies of Old Ross. If my husband John
can catch me by the hand or cloak when I ride by,
and has courage not to let go his grip, I'll be safe.
Here's the king. Don't open your mouth to answer.'

"The dark man didn't once cast his eye towards
Molly, and he seemed to have no suspicion of me.

When we came out I looked about me, and saw that we were in the dyke of the Rath of Cromogue. I was on the horse again, which was nothing but a big ragweed, and I was in dread every minute I'd fall off, but nothing happened till I found myself in my own cabin.

"The king slipped five guineas into my hand as soon as I was on the ground, and thanked me, and bade me good night. I hope I'll never see his face again. I got into bed, and couldn't sleep for a long time, and when I examined my five guineas this morning, which I left in the table drawer last night, I only found five withered leaves of oak – bad luck to the giver!"

Well, you may imagine the fright, and the joy, and the grief the poor man was in when the woman finished her story. They talked and they talked, till Friday night came, when both were standing where the mountain road crosses the one going to Ross. There they stood, looking towards the bridge of

The Fairy Wife

Thuar, in the dead of the night, with a little moonlight shining.

At last the woman gave a start, and said, "Here they come, bridles jingling and feathers tossing!" He looked, but could see nothing, and she stood trembling and her eyes wide open, looking down the way to the ford of Ballinacoola.

"I see your wife," said she, "riding on the outside. We'll walk on quietly, as if we suspected nothing, and when we are passing I'll give you a shove. If you don't do your duty then, woe be with you!"

Well, they walked on easy, their poor hearts beating hard, and though he could see nothing, he heard a faint jingle and trampling and rustling, and at last he got the push that she promised. He spread out his arms, and there was his wife's waist within them, and he could see her plain, but such a hullabulloo rose as if there was an earthquake, and he found himself surrounded by horrible-looking things, roaring at him and striving to pull his wife away. But he made the sign of the cross and bid them begone in God's name, and held his wife as if his arms were made of iron. In one moment everything was as silent as the grave, and the poor woman lay in a faint in the arms of her husband and her good neighbour. Well, all in good time she was minding her family and her business again, and I expect, after the fright she got, she spent more time praying, and avoided fairies all the days of the week, and particularly on Sunday.

Billy Beg, Tom Beg, and the Fairies

By Sophia Morrison

Not far from Dalby, two humpback cobblers called Billy Beg and Tom Beg lived together on a lonely farm. Billy Beg was cleverer than Tom Beg, who was always at his command. One day Billy gave Tom a staff, and said, "Tom Beg, go to the mountain and fetch home the white sheep."

Tom took the staff and went to the mountain, but he could not find the white sheep. At last, when he was far from home, and dusk was coming on, he began to think that he had best go back. The night was fine, and stars and a small crescent moon were in the sky. Tom was hastening home, and had almost reached Glen Rushen, when he lost his way in a grey mist. When it cleared, Tom found himself in a green glen he had never seen before, though he knew every glen within five miles of him. He was wondering where he could be, when he heard a faraway sound drawing nearer to him.

"Aw," said he to himself, "there's more than myself afoot on the mountains tonight."

The sound grew louder. First, it was like the humming of bees, then like rushing water, and last it was like the marching of a crowd. All of a sudden the glen was full of fine horses and little people riding on them, with the lights on their red caps shining like the stars above. There was the blowing of horns, the waving of flags, and the playing of music. Tom thought that he had never seen

anything so splendid as all he saw there. In the
midst of the drilling and dancing, he saw coming
towards him the grandest little man he had ever set
eyes upon, dressed in gold and silver silk, shining
like a raven's wing.

"It is a bad time you have chosen to come this way," said the little man, who was the king.

"It is not here that I'm wishing to be," said Tom.

The king said, "Are you one of us tonight, Tom?"

"I am surely," said Tom.

"Then," said the king, "it will be your duty to take the password. You must stand at the foot of the glen, and as each regiment goes by, you must take the password – it is: 'Monday, Tuesday, Wednesday, Thursday, Friday, Saturday.'"

"I'll do that with a heart and a half," said Tom.

At daybreak the fiddlers took up their fiddles, the fairy army set itself in order, the fiddlers played before them out of the glen, and sweet that music was. Each regiment gave the password to Tom as it went by, "Monday, Tuesday, Wednesday, Thursday, Friday, Saturday."

Last of all came the king, and he, too, gave it, "Monday, Tuesday, Wednesday, Thursday, Friday, Saturday."

Billy Beg, Tom Beg, and the Fairies

Then he called to one of his men, "Take the hump from this fellow's back," and before the words were out of his mouth the hump was whisked off Tom Beg's back and thrown into the hedge.

How proud was Tom, who now found himself the straightest man in the Isle of Man! He went back down the mountain and came home early in the morning with a light heart and an eager step. Billy was amazed when he saw Tom standing so straight and strong, and when Tom had rested and refreshed himself he told his story about how he had met the fairies who came every night to Glen Rushen to drill.

The next night Billy set off along the mountain road and came at last to the green glen. About midnight he heard the trampling of horses, the lashing of whips, and a great hullabaloo, and, behold, the fairies and their king all at drill in the glen as Tom had said.

When they saw the humpback they all stopped.

One came forward and crossly asked his business.

"I am one of yourselves for the night, and should be glad to do you some service," said Billy.

So he was set to take the password, 'Monday, Tuesday, Wednesday, Thursday, Friday, Saturday.' And at daybreak the King said, "It's time for us to be off," and up came regiment after regiment giving Billy the password, "Monday, Tuesday, Wednesday, Thursday, Friday, Saturday."

Last of all came the king with his men. and gave the password also, "Monday, Tuesday, Wednesday, Thursday, Friday, Saturday."

"And Sunday," said Billy, thinking himself clever. Then there was a great outcry.

"Get the hump that was taken off that fellow's back last night and put it on this man's back," said the king, with flashing eyes, pointing to the hump that lay under the hedge.

Before the words were well out of his mouth the hump was clapped onto Billy's back.

"Now," said the king, "be off, and if ever I find
you here again, we will clap another hump onto
your front!"

And they all marched away with one great shout,
and left poor Billy standing where they had found
him, with a hump growing on each shoulder. And he
came home next day dragging one foot after another,
with a wizened face as cross as two sticks, with his
two humps on his back, and if they are not off they
are there still.

Fairy
Ointment

By Joseph Jacobs

Dame Goody was a nurse who looked after sick people, and minded babies. One night she woke up at midnight, and when she went downstairs, she saw a strange, little old fellow, who asked her to come to his wife who was too ill to mind her baby. Although Dame Goody didn't like the look of the old fellow, she decided that business is business, so she popped on her things, and went down to him. And when she got down to him, he whisked her up on to a large coal-black horse with fiery eyes, that stood at the door, and soon they were going at a rare pace, Dame Goody holding on to the old fellow like grim death.

They rode and they rode, till at last they stopped before a cottage door. There they got down and went in and found the good woman in bed with the children playing about, and the baby, a fine bouncing boy, beside her.

Dame Goody took the baby, which was as fine a boy as you'd wish to see. The mother, when she handed the baby to Dame Goody to mind, gave her a box of ointment, and told her to stroke the baby's eyes with it as soon as it opened them.

After a while it began to open its eyes. Dame Goody saw that it had eyes just like its father. So she took the box of ointment and stroked its two eyelids with it. But she couldn't help wondering what it was for, as she had never seen such a thing done before. So she looked to see if the others were looking, and, when they were not noticing, she stroked her own right eyelid with the ointment.

No sooner had she done so, than everything seemed changed about her. The cottage became elegantly furnished. The mother in the bed was a beautiful lady, dressed up in white silk. The little baby was still more beautiful than before, and its clothes were made of a sort of silvery gauze.

Its little brothers and sisters around the bed were flat-nosed imps with pointed ears, who made faces at one another, and scratched their heads. In fact, they were up to all kinds of mischief, and Dame Goody knew that she had got into a house of fairies. But she said nothing, and as soon as the lady was well enough to mind the baby, she asked the old fellow to take her back home. So he came round to the door with the coal-black horse with eyes of fire, and off they went as fast as before till they came to Dame Goody's cottage, where the strange fellow lifted her down and left her, thanking her civilly enough, and paying her more than she had ever been paid before for such service.

Now next day happened to be market day, and as Dame Goody had been away from home, she wanted many things in the house, and trudged off to get them at the market. As she was buying the things she wanted, who should she see but the strange fellow who had taken her on the coal-black horse. And what do you think he was doing? Why he went about from stall to stall taking things from each – here some fruit, and there some eggs, and so on – and no one seemed to take any notice.

Now Dame Goody did not think it her business to interfere, but she thought she ought not to let so good a customer pass without speaking. So she went up to him, bobbed a curtsey and said, "Good day, sir, I hope your good lady and the little one are as well as—"

But she couldn't finish what she was saying, for the funny old fellow started back in surprise, and he said to her, "What! Do you see me today?"

"See you," said she, "why, of course I do, as plain as the sun in the skies, and what's more," said she, "I see you are busy, too, into the bargain."

"Ah, you see too much," said he, "now, pray, with

which eye do you see all this?"

"With the right eye to be sure," said she, as proud as can be to find him out.

"The ointment! The ointment!" cried the old fairy thief. "Take that for meddling with what don't concern you – you shall see me no more." And with that he struck her on the right eye, and she couldn't see him anymore, and, what was worse, she could no longer see with her right eye from that hour until this.

Murdoch's Rath

By Juliana Horatia Gatty Ewing

A rath is an ancient hillfort, which looks like a grassy mound on top of a high bank. They are scattered all over Ireland and fairies are believed to live inside them.

*T*here was not a nicer boy in all Ireland than Pat, and clever at his trade too, if only he'd had one.

But from his cradle he learnt nothing (small blame to him with no one to teach him!), so when he grew old enough to make his own decisions, he earned his living by running errands for his neighbours. Pat proved that he could always be trusted to make the best of a bad bargain, and bring back all the change, for he was the soul of honesty and good nature.

It's no wonder then that he was beloved by everyone, and got as much work as he could do, and if the pay had fitted the work, he'd have been mighty comfortable. But as it was, what he got wouldn't have kept him in shoe leather, if it wasn't for the fact that he made ends meet by keeping his shoes in his pocket, except when he was in the town and obliged to look genteel for the credit of the place he came from.

Well, all was going on as peacefully as could be, till one market day, when business (or it may have been pleasure) detained him till the very end of the evening, and by nightfall, when he began to make the journey home, he never thought to leave off his shoes, but tramped on just as if shoe leather were made to be knocked to bits on the king's highway.

And as he walked this was what he was saying to himself: "A dozen hanks of grey yarn for Mistress Murphy, three gross of bright buttons for the tailor, half an ounce of throat drops for Father Andrew, and an ounce of snuff for his housekeeper," and so on, over and over. For these were what he went to the town to fetch, and he was afraid one of the lot might have slipped his memory.

Now everybody knows there are two ways home from the town – the highway, and the way by Murdoch's Rath.

Murdoch's Rath was a pleasant enough spot to stroll along during the daytime, but not many people cared to walk past it when the sun was down. And in all the years Pat was walking backwards and forwards, he never once came home except by the high road till this unlucky evening, when, just at the place where the two roads part, he got, as one may say, into a sort of confusion. How far he walked he never could tell, before all of a sudden the moon shone out from behind the clouds as bright as day, and Pat found himself in Murdoch's Rath. And this was only the smallest part of the wonder, for the Rath was full of fairies.

When Pat saw them they were dancing round and round in circles. It made his feet tingle to look at them, for he was a good dancer himself. As he sat on the side of the Rath, and snapped his fingers to mark the time, the dancing stopped, and a little man came up to Pat. He wore a tall black hat and a fine green coat, with white stockings, and red shoes on his tiny feet.

"Won't you take a turn with us, Pat?" said he, bowing till he nearly touched the ground. And, indeed, he had not far to go, for he was barely two feet high.

"You don't need to say it twice, sir," said Pat. "I will be proud to take to the the floor with ye," and before you could look round, there was Pat in the circle dancing away with all his might.

At first his feet felt like feathers for lightness, and it seemed as if he could have gone on forever. But at last he grew tired, and would have liked to stop, but the fairies would not, and so they danced on and on. Pat tried to think of something good to say, that he might free himself from the spell, but all he could think of was, 'A dozen hanks of grey yarn for Mistress Murphy, three gross of bright buttons for the tailor, half an ounce of throat drops for Father Andrew, and an ounce of snuff for his housekeeper,' and so on.

And it seemed to Pat that the moon was on the one side of the Rath when they began to dance, and on the other side when they left off, but he could not be sure after all that going round. One thing was plain enough. He danced every bit of leather off the soles of his feet, and they were blistered so that he could hardly stand, but all the little folk did was

VISITORS TO FAIRYLAND

to stand and hold their sides with laughing at him.

At last the one who spoke before stepped up to him. "Don't break your heart about it, Pat," said he. "I'll lend you my shoes till the morning, for you seem to be a good natured boy."

Well, Pat looked at the fairy man's shoes, which were the size of a baby's, and he looked at his own feet, but not wishing to be uncivil, "Thank ye kindly, sir," said he. "And if you'll be good enough to put them on for me, maybe you won't spoil the shape." For he thought to himself, 'Small blame to me if the little gentleman can't get them to fit.'

With that he sat down on the side of the Rath, and the fairy man put on the shoes for him. As soon as they touched Pat's feet they became altogether a convenient size, and fitted him like wax. And, more than that, when he stood up, he didn't feel his blisters at all.

"Bring 'em back to the Rath at sunrise, Pat, my boy," said the little man. And as Pat was climbing over the ditch, "Look round, Pat," said he. And when Pat looked round, there were jewels and pearls lying at the roots of the bushes on the ditch, as thick as peas.

"Will you help yourself, or take what's given ye, Pat?" said the fairy man.

"Did I ever learn manners?" said Pat. "Would you have me help myself before company? I'll take what your honour pleases to give me, and I'll be thankful for it."

The fairy man picked a lot of yellow blossoms from the bushes, and filled Pat's pockets.

"Keep 'em for love, Pat, me darling" said he.

Pat would have liked some of the jewels, but he put the blossoms by for love.

VISITORS TO FAIRYLAND

"Good evening to your honour," said he.

"And where are you going, Pat, dear?" said the fairy man.

"I'm going home," said Pat. And if the fairy man didn't know where that was, small blame to him.

"Just let me dust them shoes for ye, Pat," said the fairy man. And as Pat lifted up each foot he breathed on it, and dusted it with the tail of his green coat.

"Home!" said he, and when he let go, Pat was at his own doorstep before he could look round, and his parcels safe and sound with him.

Next morning he was up with the sun, and carried the fairy man's shoes back to the Rath. As he came up, the little man looked over the ditch.

"The top of the morning to your honour," said Pat, "here's your shoes."

"You're an honest boy, Pat," said the little gentleman. "It's inconvenienced I am without them, for I have only the one pair. Have you looked at the

296

yellow flowers this morning?" he said.

"I have not, sir," said Pat, "I'd be loth to deceive you. I came off as soon as I was up."

"Be sure to look when you get back, Pat," said the fairy man, "and good luck to ye."

With that he disappeared, and Pat went home. He looked for the blossoms, as the fairy man told him, and there's not a word of truth in this tale if they weren't all pure gold pieces.

Well, now Pat was so rich, he went to the shoemaker to order another pair of brogues. Being a kindly, gossiping boy, the shoemaker soon learnt the whole story of the fairy man and the Rath. This stirred up the shoemaker's greed, and he resolved to go the next night himself, to see if he could not dance with the fairies, and have the same luck.

He found his way to the Rath, and sure enough the fairies were dancing, and asked him to join. He danced the soles off his brogues, as Pat did, and the fairy man lent him his shoes, and sent him home in a twinkling.

As he was going over the ditch, he looked round, and saw the roots of the bushes glowing with precious stones as if they had been glow worms.

"Will you help yourself, or take what's given ye?" said the fairy man.

"I'll help myself, if you please," said the cobbler, for he thought, 'If I can't get more than Pat brought home, my fingers must all be thumbs.'

So he drove his hand into the bushes, and if he didn't get plenty, it wasn't for want of grasping.

When he got up in the morning, he went straight to look at the jewels. But not a stone of the lot was more precious than roadside pebbles. "I ought not to look till I come back from the Rath," said he. "It's best to do like Pat."

But he made up his mind not to return the fairy man's shoes. "Who knows the virtue that's in them?" he said. So he made a small pair of red leather shoes, as like as could be to the pair he had borrowed, and he blacked the others upon his feet, so that the fairies might not know them, and at sunrise he went to the Rath.

The fairy man was looking over the ditch, just as he had done before.

"Good morning to you," said he.

"The top of the morning to you, sir," said the cobbler. "Here's your shoes." And he handed him the pair that he had made, making sure that his face was as grave as a judge.

The fairy man looked at them, but he said nothing, though he did not put them on. "Have you looked at the things you got last night?" said he.

"I'll not deceive you, sir," said the cobbler. "I came to see you as soon as I was up. Not a peep I took at them."

"Be sure to look when you get back," said the fairy man. And just as the cobbler was getting over the ditch to go home, he said, "If my eyes don't deceive me," said he, "there's a little dirt on your left shoe. Let me dust it with the tail of my coat."

'That means home in a twinkling,' thought the cobbler, and he held up his foot.

The fairy man dusted it, and muttered something the cobbler did not hear. "It's the dirty pastures that you've come through," said he, "for the other shoe's as bad."

So the cobbler held up his right foot, and the fairy man rubbed that with the tail of his green coat.

When all was done the cobbler's feet seemed to tingle, and then to itch, and then to smart, and then to burn. And at last he began to dance, and he danced all round the Rath (the fairy man laughing and holding his sides), and then round and round again. And he danced till he cried out with weariness, and tried to shake the shoes off. But they stuck fast, and the fairies drove him over the ditch, and through the bushes, and he danced away.

Where he danced to, I cannot tell you. Whether he ever got rid of the fairy shoes, I do not know. The

Murdoch's Rath

jewels never were more than wayside pebbles, and they were swept out when his cabin was cleaned, which was not too soon, you may be sure.

All this happened long ago, but there are those who say that the covetous cobbler dances still, between sunset and sunrise, round Murdoch's Rath.

I WISH, I WISH

Beautiful
as the Day

From *Five Children and It*
by E Nesbit

The house was three miles from the station, but
before the dusty hired carriage had rattled
along for five minutes the children began to put
their heads out of the window to say, "Aren't we
nearly there?" And every time they passed a house,
which was not very often, they all said, "Oh, is *this*
it?" But it never was, till they reached the very top of
the hill, just past the chalk quarry and before you

Beautiful as the Day

come to the gravel pit. And then there was a white house with a green garden and an orchard beyond, and mother said, "Here we are!"

"How white the house is," said Robert.

"And look at the roses," said Anthea.

"And the plums," said Jane.

"It is rather decent," Cyril admitted.

The baby said, "Wanty go walky."

Everyone got their legs kicked or their feet trodden on in the scramble to get out of the carriage that very minute, but no one seemed to mind. The children had explored the gardens and the outhouses thoroughly before they were caught and cleaned for tea, and they saw quite well that they were certain to be happy at the White House. The best part of it all was that there were no rules about not going to places and not doing things. In London almost everything is labelled 'You mustn't touch', and though the label is invisible, it's just as bad, because you know it's there.

I WISH, I WISH

Now that I have begun to tell you about the place, I feel that I could go on and make this into a most interesting story about all the ordinary things that the children did – just the kind of things you do yourself, you know – and you would believe every word of it. But children will believe almost anything, and I daresay you will find it quite easy to believe that before Anthea and Cyril and the others had been a week in the country they had found a fairy. At least they called it that, because that was what it called itself, but it was not at all like any fairy read about.

It was at the gravel pits. Father had to go away suddenly on business, and mother had gone away to stay with Granny, who was not very well. They both went in a great hurry, and when they were gone the house seemed dreadfully quiet and empty. It was Cyril who said, "I say, let's take our spades and go and dig in the gravel pits. We can pretend we're all at the seaside."

Beautiful as the Day

"Father said it was once," Anthea said, "he says there are shells there thousands of years old."

So they went. Of course they had been to the edge of the gravel pit and looked over, but they had not gone down into it for fear father should say they mustn't play there.

Each of the children carried its own spade, and took it in turns to carry the Lamb. He was the baby, and they called him that because 'Baa' was the first thing he ever said. They called Anthea 'Panther',

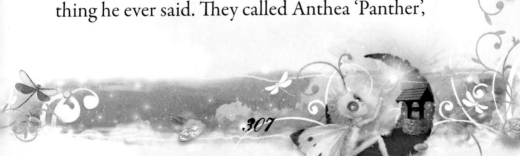

which sounds silly when you read it, but when you say it it sounds a little like her name.

First the children built a castle, of course, but castle-building is rather poor fun when you have no hope of the tide ever coming in to fill the moat.

Cyril wanted to dig out a cave to play smugglers in, but the others thought it might bury them alive, so it ended in all spades going to work together to dig a hole to Australia. The children dug and they dug and they dug, and their hands got sandy and hot and red, and their faces got damp and shiny. The Lamb had tried to eat the sand, and had cried so hard when he found that it was not – as he had supposed – brown sugar, that he was now tired out, and was lying asleep in a warm fat bunch in the middle of the half-finished castle. This left his brothers and sisters free to work really hard, and the hole that was to come out in Australia soon grew so deep that Jane (who was called Pussy for short) begged the others to stop.

Beautiful as the Day

Cyril and Anthea knew that Australia was not quite so near as all that, but they agreed to stop using the spades and go on with their hands. This was quite easy, because the sand at the bottom of the hole was very soft and fine and dry, like sea sand.

The party were just making up their minds that sand makes you thirstier when it is not by the seaside, and someone had suggested going home for lemonade, when Anthea suddenly screamed, "Cyril! Come here! Oh, come quick! It's alive! It'll get away! Quick!"

They all hurried back.

"Perhaps it is a snake," said Jane, shuddering.

"Oh, don't be silly!" said Anthea, "it's not a snake. It's got feet, I saw them, and fur! No – not the spade. You'll hurt it! Dig with your hands."

But Cyril merely observed that his sister must have gone off her nut, and he and Robert dug with spades while Anthea sat on the edge of the hole, jumping up and down with hotness and anxiety.

I WISH, I WISH

They dug carefully, and presently everyone could see that there really was something moving in the bottom of the hole.

Then Anthea cried out, "*I'm* not afraid. Let me dig," and fell on her knees and began to scratch like a dog does when he has suddenly remembered where it was that he buried his bone.

"Oh, I felt fur," she cried, half laughing and half crying. "I did indeed! I did!" Suddenly a dry husky voice in the sand made them all jump back, and their hearts jumped nearly as fast as they did.

"Leave me alone," it said. Everyone heard the voice and looked at the others to see if they had too.

"But we want to see you," said Robert bravely.

"I wish you'd come out," said Anthea, also taking courage.

"Oh, well – if that's your wish," the voice said, and the sand stirred and spun, and something brown and furry came rolling out into the hole and the sand fell off it, and it sat there yawning.

310

Beautiful as the Day

"I believe I must have dropped asleep," it said, stretching itself.

The children stood round the hole in a ring, looking at the creature they had found. It was certainly worth looking at. Its eyes were on long horns like a snail's eyes, and it could move them in and out like telescopes. It had ears like a bat's ears, and its tubby body was shaped like a spider's and

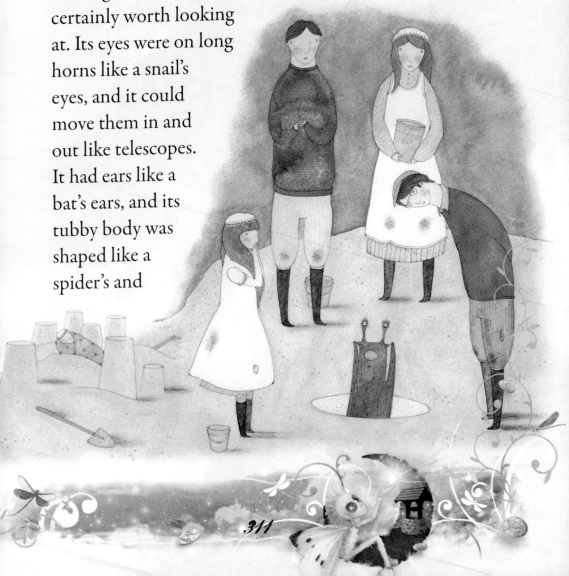

covered with thick soft fur. Its legs and arms were furry too, and it had hands and feet like a monkey's.

"What on earth is it?" Jane said in amazement. "Shall we take it home?"

The thing turned its long eyes to look at her, and said, "Does she always talk nonsense, or is it only the rubbish on her head that makes her silly?"

It looked scornfully at Jane's hat as it spoke.

"She doesn't mean to be silly," Anthea said gently, "We none of us do, whatever you may think. Don't be frightened."

It said. "*Me* frightened? Upon my word! Why, you talk as if I were nobody in particular." All its fur stood out like a cat's when it is going to fight.

"Well," said Anthea, still kindly, "perhaps if we knew who you are in particular we could think of something to say that wouldn't make you cross."

"You don't know?" it said. "Well, I knew the world had changed – but – well, really – do you mean to tell me seriously you don't know a

312

Beautiful as the Day

Psammead when you see one? Or, in plain English, then, a *sand-fairy*. Don't you know a sand-fairy when you see one?"

Of course no one could think of anything to say, but at last Robert thought of 'How long have you lived here?' and he said it at once.

"Oh, ages – several thousand years," replied the Psammead.

"Was the world like this then?"

It stopped digging.

"Not a bit," it said, "it was nearly all sand where I lived, and coal grew on trees. We sand-fairies used to live on the seashore, and the children used to come with their little flint-spades and flint-pails and make castles for us to live in. That's thousands of years ago, but I hear that children still build castles on the sand. It's hard to break yourself of a habit."

"Why did you stop living in castles?" asked Robert, with interest.

"It's a sad story," said the Psammead gloomily.

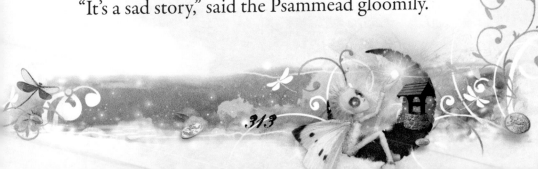

315

"It was because they *would* build moats to the castles, and the nasty wet bubbling sea used to come in, and of course as soon as a sand-fairy got wet it caught cold, and generally died. And so there got to be fewer and fewer."

"And did *you* get wet?" Robert inquired.

The sand-fairy shuddered. "Only once," it said, "the end of the twelfth hair of my top left whisker – I feel the place still in damp weather. I scurried away to the back of the beach, and dug myself a house deep in warm dry sand, and there I've been ever since. And the sea changed its lodgings afterwards. And now I'm not going to tell you another thing."

"Just one more, please," said the children. "Can you give wishes now?"

"Of course," said it, "didn't I give you yours a few minutes ago? You said, 'I wish you'd come out,' and I did."

"Oh, please, mayn't we have another?"

"Yes, but be quick about it. I'm tired of you."

Beautiful as the Day

I daresay you have often thought what you would do if you had three wishes given you. These children had often talked this matter over, but, now the chance had suddenly come to them, they could not make up their minds.

"Quick," said the sand-fairy crossly.

No one could think of anything. Only Anthea did manage to remember a private wish of her own and Jane's which they had never told the boys. "I wish we were all as beautiful as the day," she said in a great hurry.

The children looked at each other, but each could see that the others were not any better looking than usual. The Psammead pushed out its long eyes, and seemed to be holding its breath and swelling itself out till it was twice as fat and furry as before. Suddenly it let its breath go in a long sigh.

"I'm really afraid I can't manage it," it said apologetically, "I must be out of practise."

The children were horribly disappointed.

"Oh, *do* try again!" they said.

"Well," said the sand-fairy, "the fact is, I was keeping back a little strength to give the rest of you your wishes with. If you'll be contented with one wish a day amongst the lot of you I daresay I can screw myself up to it. Do you agree to that?"

"Yes, oh yes!" they all agreed.

It stretched out its eyes farther than ever, and swelled and swelled and swelled.

"I do hope it won't hurt itself," said Anthea.

"Or crack its skin," Robert said anxiously.

Everyone was very much relieved when the sand-fairy, after getting so big that it almost filled up the hole in the sand, suddenly let out its breath and went back to its proper size.

"That's all right," it said, panting heavily. "It'll come easier tomorrow. It'll last till sunset."

"Did it hurt much?" asked Anthea.

"Only my whisker, thank you," said he.

And with a hurried 'Good day!' the sand-fairy

Beautiful as the Day

scratched suddenly with its hands and feet, and disappeared in the sand. Then the children looked at each other, and each child suddenly found itself alone with three strangers, all radiantly beautiful.

They stood for some moments in perfect silence. Each thought that its brothers and sisters had wandered off, and that these strange children had stolen up while it was watching the sand-fairy.

Anthea spoke first, "Excuse me," she said very politely to Jane, who now had enormous blue eyes and a cloud of russet hair, "but have you seen two little boys and a little girl anywhere about?"

"I was just going to ask you that," said Jane.

And then Cyril cried, "Why, it's *you*! I know the hole in your pinafore! You *are* Jane, aren't you? Crikey! The wish has come off, after all. I say, am I as handsome as you are?"

"If you're Cyril, I liked you better before," said Anthea decidedly. "You look like the picture of the young chorister, with your golden hair, you'll die

317

young, I shouldn't wonder. And if that's Robert,
he's like an Italian organ grinder."

"You two girls are like silly Christmas cards, then
– that's all," said Robert angrily.

"Well, it's no use finding fault with each other,"
said Anthea, "let's get the Lamb and lug it home to
dinner. The servants will admire us most awfully,
you'll see."

Baby was just waking when
they got to him. The children
were relieved to find that he
was not as beautiful as the day,
but just the same as usual.

"I suppose he's too
young to have wishes," said
Jane. "We shall have to
mention him specially
next time."

Anthea ran forward
and held out her arms.

Beautiful as the Day

"Come to own Panther, ducky," she said.

The Baby looked at her disapprovingly, and put a sandy pink thumb in his mouth.

"G'way long!" said the Baby.

"Come to own Pussy," said Jane.

"Wants my Panty," said the Lamb dismally.

"Here, come on, Veteran," said Robert, "come and have a yidey on Yobby's back."

"Yah, narky narky boy," howled the Baby, giving way altogether. Then the children knew the worst: *The baby did not know them!*

I WISH, I WISH

They all looked at each other in despair, and it was terrible to each, in this dire emergency, to meet only the beautiful eyes of perfect strangers, instead of the merry, friendly, little eyes of its own brothers and sisters.

"This is most truly awful," said Cyril. "I can't carry him home with him screaming like that. Fancy having to make friends with our own baby! It's just too silly."

That, however, was exactly what they had to do. It took them over an hour to persuade the Lamb that they were not dangerous strangers. This difficult task was not rendered any easier by the fact that he was by this time as hungry as a lion and as thirsty as a desert.

At last he consented to allow these peculiar people to carry him home by turns, but as he refused to hold on to such new acquaintances he was a dead weight and most exhausting.

"Thank goodness, we're home!" said Jane,

staggering through the iron gate to where Martha, the nursemaid, stood at the front door shading her eyes with her hand and looking out anxiously. "Here! Do take baby!"

Martha snatched the baby from her arms.

"Thanks be, *he's* safe back," she said. "Where are the others, and whoever to goodness gracious are all of you?'

"We're *us*, of course," said Robert.

"And who's *us*, when you're at home?" asked Martha scornfully.

"I know we *look* different, but I'm Anthea, and we're so tired, and it's long past dinner time."

"Then go home to your dinners, whoever you are, and if our children put you up to this play-acting you can tell them from me they'll catch it, so they know what to expect!"

With that she did bang the door, leaving them all outside. Cyril rang the bell violently. No answer. Presently cook put her head out of a bedroom window and said, "If you don't take yourselves off, I'll go and fetch the police." And she slammed down the window.

"It's no good," said Anthea. "Oh, do, do come away before we get sent to prison!"

The boys said it was nonsense, and the law of England couldn't put you in prison for just being as beautiful as the day, but all the same they followed the others out into the lane.

"We shall be our proper selves after sunset, I suppose," said Jane.

It was a horrible afternoon. There was no house near where the children could beg a crust of bread or even a glass of water. They were afraid to go to the village, because they had seen Martha go down there with a basket, and there was a local constable. True, they were all as beautiful as the day, but that is a poor comfort when you are as hungry as a hunter and as thirsty as a sponge.

It came at last to their sitting down in a row

Beautiful as the Day

under the hedge, with their feet in a dry ditch, waiting for sunset.

At last hunger and fright and crossness and tiredness – four very nasty things – all joined together to bring one nice thing, and that was sleep. The children lay asleep in a row, with their beautiful eyes shut and their beautiful mouths open. Anthea woke first. The sun had set, and the twilight was coming on.

"Wake up," she said, almost in tears of joy, "it's all right. Oh, Cyril, how nice and ugly you do look, with your old freckles and your brown hair and your little eyes. And so do you all!" she added, so that they might not feel jealous.

When they got home they were very much scolded by Martha, who told them about the strange children.

"A good-looking lot, I must say, but that impudent."

"I know," said Robert, who knew by bitter

323

experience how hopeless it would be to try to explain things to Martha.

"And where on earth have you been all this time, you naughty little things, you?"

"In the lane."

"Why didn't you come home hours ago?"

"We couldn't because of *them*," said Anthea. "They wouldn't let us go."

"'Who?"

"The children who were as beautiful as the day. They kept us there till after sunset. We couldn't come back till they'd gone. You don't know how we hated them! Oh, do, do give us some supper – we are so hungry."

"Hungry! I should think so," said Martha angrily, "out all day like this. Well, I hope it'll be a lesson to you not to go picking up with strange children – down here after measles, as likely as not! Now mind, if you see them again, don't you speak to them – not one word."

Beautiful as the Day

"If ever we *do* see them again we'll tell you," Anthea said, and Robert, fixing his eyes fondly on the cold beef that was being brought in on a tray by cook, added in heartfelt undertones, "And we'll take jolly good care we never *do* see them again."

And they never have.

Christmas
Every Day

By W D Howells

*T*he little girl came into her papa's study and
asked for a story. He tried to beg off, for he
was busy, but she would not let him. So he began,
"Well, once there was a little pig—"

But the little girl said that she had heard pig
stories till she was sick of them.

"Well, what kind of story shall I tell, then?"

"About Christmas. It's getting to be the season.

Christmas Every Day

After all, it's past Thanksgiving already."

"It seems to me," her papa argued, "that I've told as often about Christmas as I have about little pigs."

"Christmas is more interesting."

"Well, then, I'll tell you about the little girl that wanted it to be Christmas every day in the year. How do you like the sound of that?"

"First-rate!" said the little girl, and she nestled into a comfortable shape in his lap, ready for listening.

"Once there was a little girl who liked Christmas so much that she wanted it to be Christmas every day. As soon as Thanksgiving was over she began to send letters to the Christmas Fairy to ask if she could make it so, and – the day before Christmas – she got a letter from the fairy, telling her that she would grant her wish to have Christmas every day for a year, and they could see how they got on.

"The little girl was a good deal excited already, preparing for the old-fashioned, once-a-year Christmas that was coming the next day, and perhaps the fairy's promise didn't make such an impression on her as it would have made at some other time. She just resolved to keep it to herself, and surprise everybody with it as it kept coming true, and then it slipped out of her mind altogether.

"She had a splendid Christmas. She went to bed early, so as to let Santa Claus have a chance at the stockings, and in the morning she was up the first of anybody and went and felt them, and found hers all lumpy with packages of candy, and oranges and grapes, and books and rubber balls, and all kinds of small presents. Then she waited around till the rest of the family were up, and she was the first to burst into the library when the doors were opened, and

look at the large presents laid out – books, and boxes of stationery, and dolls, and little stoves, and skates, and photograph-frames, and little easels, and boxes of water-colours, and Turkish paste, and nougat, and candied cherries, and dolls' houses – and the big Christmas tree, lighted and standing in a basket in the middle.

"She had a splendid Christmas all day. She ate so much candy that she did not want any breakfast, and she went round giving the presents she had got for other people, and came home and ate turkey and cranberry for dinner, and plum-pudding and nuts and raisins and oranges and more candy, and then went out sledging, and came in with a stomach-ache, crying, and her papa said he would see if his house was turned into that sort of fool's paradise another year, and they had a light supper, and pretty early everybody went to bed cross.

"The little girl slept very heavily, and she slept very late, but she was wakened at last by the other

children dancing round her bed with their
stockings full of presents in their hands.

"'What is it?' said the little girl, and she rubbed
her eyes and tried to sit up in bed.

"'Christmas! Christmas! Christmas!' they all
shouted, and waved their stockings.

"'Nonsense! It was Christmas yesterday.'

"Her brothers and sisters just laughed. 'We don't
know about that. It's Christmas today, anyway. You
come into the library and see.'

"Then all at once it flashed on the little girl that
the fairy was keeping her promise, and her year of
Christmases was beginning. She was dreadfully
sleepy, but she sprang up like a lark – a lark that had
overeaten itself and gone to bed cross – and darted
into the library. There it was again! Books, and
boxes of stationery..."

"'You needn't go over it all, papa, I guess I can
remember just what was there," said the little girl.

"Well, and there was the Christmas tree blazing

away, and the family picking out their presents, but looking pretty sleepy, and her father perfectly puzzled, and her mother ready to cry.

"'I don't see how I'm to dispose of all these things,' said her mother, and her father said it seemed to him they had had something just like it the day before, but he supposed he must have dreamt it. This struck the little girl as the best kind joke, and so she ate so much candy she didn't want breakfast, and went round carrying presents, and had turkey and cranberry for dinner, and then went out sledging, and came in with a…"

"Papa!"

"Well, what now?"

"What did you promise, you forgetful thing?"

"Oh! Oh yes!

"Well, the next day, it was just the same thing over again, but everybody getting crosser, and at the end of a week's time so many people had lost their tempers that you could pick up lost tempers anywhere, they perfectly strewed the ground. Even when people tried to recover their tempers they usually got somebody else's, and it made the most dreadful mix.

"The little girl began to get frightened, keeping the secret all to herself. She wanted to tell her mother, but she didn't dare to, and she was ashamed to ask the fairy to take back her gift, it seemed ungrateful and ill-bred, and she thought she would try to stand it, but she hardly knew how she could, for a whole year. So it went on and on, and it was Christmas on St Valentine's Day and Washington's birthday, just the same as any day, and it didn't skip even the first of April, though everything was counterfeit that day, and that was some little relief.

"After a while turkeys got to be about a thousand dollars apiece and they got to passing off almost anything for turkeys – half-grown humming-birds, and even rocs out of the Arabian Nights – the real turkeys were so scarce. And cranberries – well, they asked a diamond apiece for cranberries. All the woods and orchards were cut down for Christmas trees, and where the woods and orchards used to be it looked just like a stubble field, with the stumps.

"After a while they had to make Christmas trees out of rags, and stuff them with bran, like old-fashioned dolls, but there were plenty of rags, because people had all got so poor, buying presents for one another, that they couldn't get any new clothes, and they just wore their old ones to tatters. They got so poor that everybody had to go to the poorhouse, except the confectioners, and the shopkeepers, and the picture-book sellers, and they all got so rich and proud that they would hardly wait upon a person when he came to buy. It was perfectly shameful!

"Well, after it had gone on for about three or four months, the little girl, whenever she came into the room in the morning and saw those great ugly, lumpy stockings dangling at the fireplace, and the disgusting presents around everywhere, used to just sit down and burst out crying. In six months she was perfectly exhausted. She couldn't even cry anymore. About the beginning of October she took to sitting down on dolls wherever she found them because she hated the sight of them so much, and by Thanksgiving she was crazy, and just slammed her presents across the room.

"By that time people didn't carry presents around nicely any more. They flung them over the fence, or through the window, or anything, and they used to write in the gift books, 'Take it, you horrid old thing!' and then go and bang it against the front door. Nearly everybody had built barns to hold their presents, but very soon the barns overflowed, and then people just let their presents lie out in the rain, or anywhere. Sometimes the police used to come and tell them to shovel their presents off the sidewalk, or they would arrest them.

"Well, before Thanksgiving came it had leaked

out who had caused all these Christmases. The little girl had suffered so much that she had talked about it in her sleep, and after that hardly anybody would play with her. People just perfectly despised her, because if it had not been for her greediness it wouldn't have happened

"When it came to Thanksgiving, and she wanted everybody to go to church, and have squash-pie and turkey, and show their gratitude, everyone said that all the turkeys had been eaten up for her old Christmas dinners, and if she would only put a stop to the Christmases, they would see about the gratitude. Wasn't it dreadful?

"And the very next day the little girl began to write letters and send them to the Christmas Fairy, and then telegrams, asking her to stop it. But it didn't do any good. And then she got to calling at the fairy's house, but the girl that came to the door always said, 'Not at home,' or 'Engaged,' or 'At dinner,' or something like that.

Christmas Every Day

"And so it went on till it came to the old once-a-year Christmas Eve. The little girl fell asleep, and when she woke up in the morning..."

"She found it was all nothing but a dream," suggested the little girl.

"No, indeed!" said her papa. "The situation was every bit as true and dreadful as it had been when she went to bed!"

"Well, what did she find out, then?"

"Why, that it wasn't Christmas at last, and wasn't

ever going to be, any more. And now it's time for us to have breakfast."

The little girl held her papa fast around the neck. "You shan't go if you're going to leave it so!"

"How do you want it left?"

"Christmas once a year."

"All right," said her papa, and he went on again...

"Well, there was the greatest rejoicing all over the country, and it extended clear up into Canada. The people met together everywhere, and hugged and kissed and cried for joy. The city carts went around town and gathered up all the chocolates and sweets and raisins and nuts, and dumped them into the river, and it made the fish perfectly sick, and the whole United States, as far out as Alaska, was one blaze of bonfires, where the children were burning up their gift books and presents of all kinds. They had the best time!

"The little girl went to thank the fairy because she had stopped it being Christmas, and she said she hoped she would keep her promise and see that Christmas never came again. Then the fairy frowned, and asked her if she was sure she knew what she meant. The little girl asked why, and the fairy said that now she was behaving as greedily as ever, so she'd better look out.

"This made the little girl think it all over carefully again, and then she said she would be willing to have it Christmas about once in a thousand years, and then she said a hundred, and then she said ten, and at long last she got down to one. The fairy said that was the good old way that had pleased people ever since Christmas began, and she agreed.

"Then the little girl said, 'What are your shoes made of?' And the fairy said, 'Leather.' And the little girl said, 'Bargain's done forever,' and skipped off, and hippity-hopped the whole way home, she was so glad.

"How will that do?" asked the papa.

"First-rate!" said the little girl, but she hated to have the story stop, and was rather quiet. However, her mamma put her head in at the door, to ask her papa, "Are you two never coming to breakfast? What have you been telling that child?"

"Oh, just a moral tale."

The little girl caught him around the neck again. "We know! Don't you tell what, papa! Don't you tell what!"

Under the Sun

By Juliana Horatia Gatty Ewing

*O*nce upon a time there lived a farmer who was
so greedy and miserly, and so very hard in all
his dealings that, as folks say, he would skin a flint.
It is needless to say that he made it a rule never to
give nor lend.

Now, by thus scraping, and saving, and grinding
for many years, he had become almost wealthy,
though, indeed, he did not enjoy it – in fact, he was

no better fed and dressed than if he had not a single penny to bless himself with. But what vexed him sorely was that his neighbour's farm prospered in every matter much better than his own, and this, although the owner was as generous as our farmer was stingy.

Now on the lands of the generous farmer (whose name was Merryweather) there lived a fairy or hillman, who made a wager that he would both beg and borrow of the envious farmer, and out-bargain him as well.

So the fairy went one day to the mean farmer's house, and asked him if he would kindly give him half a stone of flour to make hasty pudding with. He added that if the farmer would lend him a bag to carry it into the hill, this should be returned clean and in good condition.

The farmer recognized with half an eye that this was the fairy who lived on his neighbour's estate. He had always laid the good fortune of the generous farmer to his being favoured by the fairies (rather than hard work and consideration for others), so he resolved to himself that he would treat the little man with all politeness.

"Look you," said he quietly to his wife, "this is no time to be saving half a stone of flour when we may make our fortunes at one happy stroke. I have heard my grandfather tell of a man who once lent a sack of oats to a party of fairies, and when he got it back it was filled with gold pieces. And as good measure as he gave of oats so he got of gold." Saying which, the farmer took a canvas bag to the flour bin, and began to fill it.

The fairy had sharper ears than the farmer imagined, and he smiled from ear to ear at the thought of the fun he could have. He leapt up to sit in the larder window and cried, "Give us good measure, neighbour, and you shall have anything under the sun that you like to ask for."

When the farmer heard him say this he was

345

nearly out of his wits with delight, and his hands
shook so much that the flour spilled all about the
larder floor.

"Thank you, dear sir," he said, "It's a bargain, and
I agree to it. My wife hears us agree, and is witness.
Wife! Wife!" he cried, running into the kitchen,
"I am to have anything under the sun that I choose
to ask for. I think first of asking for neighbour
Merryweather's estate, but this is a chance never
likely to happen again, and I should like to make a
wise choice."

"You will be given a week to think it over in,"
said the fairy, who had come into the kitchen
behind him. "I must be off now, so give me my
flour, and come to the hill behind your house seven
days hence at midnight."

"Not for seven days, did you say, sir? You know,
dear sir, when amongst each other we men have to
wait for the settlement of an account, we expect
something over and above the exact amount.

Interest we call it, my dear sir."

"And you want me to give you something extra for waiting a week?" asked the fairy. "And what do you expect?"

"Oh, my dear sir, I will leave it entirely to you," said the farmer, thinking himself generous.

"I will give you something over and above what you shall choose," said the fairy, "but, as you say, I shall decide what it is to be." And with this pronouncement he shouldered the flour-sack, and went his way.

For the next seven days, the farmer had no peace for thinking and scheming how to get the most out of his one wish. His wife made many suggestions to which he did not agree, but he was careful not to quarrel with her, "For," he said, "we will not be like the foolish couple who wasted three wishes on black puddings."

And so, after a week of anxious thinking, he came back to what had been his very first thought, and resolved to ask for his neighbour's estate.

At last the night came. It was full moon, and the
farmer looked anxiously about, fearing the fairy
might not be true to his appointment. But at
midnight he appeared, with the flour
bag neatly folded in his hand.

"You will keep the bargain,"
said the farmer, "of course. I
am to have anything under
the sun I ask for, and I am
to have it right now."

"Indeed you
shall – ask away,"
replied the fairy.

"I want my
neighbour
Merryweather's
whole estate," said
the farmer.

"What, all this

land below here, that joins on to your own farm?"

"Every acre," said the farmer.

"Unfortunately for you, Farmer Merryweather's fields are under the moon at present," said the fairy, coolly, "and thus not within the terms of the agreement. You must choose again."

But the farmer could choose nothing that was not then under the moon, though he thought with all his might. At once he realized that he had been outwitted, and his rage knew no bounds at the trick the fairy had played on him.

"Give me my bag, at any rate," he screamed, "and the string – and your own extra gift that you promised. For half a loaf is better than no bread," he muttered to himself, "and I may yet come in for a few gold pieces."

"There's your bag," cried the fairy, gleefully clapping it over the old miser's head like an extinguisher, "it's clean enough for a nightcap. And there's your string," he added, tying it tightly round the farmer's throat. "And, for my part, I'll now give you exactly what you deserve."

Saying which he gave the mean farmer such a hearty kick that he rolled straight down from the very top of the hill to his own back door.

"And if all that does not satisfy you, I'll give you as much again," shouted the fairy after him, and as the farmer made no reply, he went chuckling back to his hill.

The Laird and the Man of Peace

By Juliana Horatia Gatty Ewing

In Scotland, fairies were often called Daoiné Shi *(pronounced dheen-ya-shee), meaning 'men of peace'. A laird is an important landowner, always known by the name of his estate. Cairngorms are a type of smoky quartz, much prized for making jewellery, especially in Scotland, where kilt pins are often decorated with them.*

*I*n the Highlands of Scotland there once lived a Laird of Brockburn, who would not believe in fairies. Not that he bore any ill-will to the Good People, or spoke uncivilly of them. Indeed he always

The Laird and the Man of Peace

denied any feeling of disrespect towards them if they existed, saying that he was a man of peace himself, and anxious to live peaceably with whatever neighbours he had, but that till he had seen one he could not believe in them.

Now one afternoon, between Hallowmas and Yule, it chanced that the laird, being out on the hills looking for some cattle, got parted from his men and dogs and was overtaken by a mist, in which, familiar as the country was to him, he lost his way.

In vain he raised his voice high, and listened low, but no sound of man or beast came back to him through the thickening vapour.

Then night fell, and darkness was added to the fog, so that Brockburn could barely see to place his feet on a path in the gloom.

Suddenly light footsteps pattered beside him, then something brushed against him, then ran between his legs. The delighted laird was sure that his favourite collie had found him once more.

"Wow, Jock, man!" he cried, "but ye needn't run about – ye near threw me on my face. What's got into ye this night, that you should lose your way in a bit of mist?"

To this a voice from the level of his elbow replied, in piping but patronizing tones, "Never did I lose my way in a mist since the night that Finn crossed over to Ireland in the dawn of history. Eh, laird! I'm well acquainted with every little path on the hillside these hundreds of years, and I'll guide ye safe home, never fear!"

At the sound of the voice, the hairs on Brockburn's head all stood up on end, and a cold, damp chill broke out all over him that was not the fog. But, despite all that, he stoutly resisted the evidence of his senses, and only felt about him in the darkness for the collie's head to pat, crying, "Bark! Jock, my mannie, bark! Then I'll recognize your voice, ye ken. It's not canny to hear ye speak like a Christian, my wee doggie."

"I'm nae your doggie, I'm a man of peace," was the swift reply. "Don't miscall your betters, Brockburn – why will ye not believe in our existence, man?"

"Seeing's believing," said the laird, stubbornly, "but the mist's a good deal too thick for seeing this night, ye ken."

"Turn round to your left, man, and ye'll see," said the dwarf, and catching Brockburn by the arm, he twisted him swiftly round three times. When the laird stopped spinning he saw a sudden blaze of bright light pouring through the mist, and it revealed a crag of the mountain well known to the laird, and which he now recognized to be a kind of turret, or tower.

Lights shone gaily through the crevices or windows of the tower, and sounds of fiddling came forth from within. Blinded by the light, and amazed at what he saw, the laird staggered, and was silent. Then stepping up to the door of the tower, the

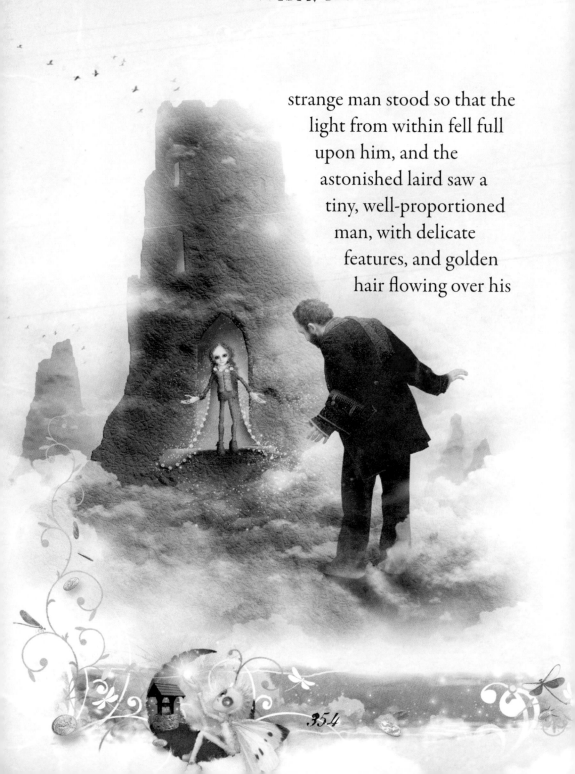

strange man stood so that the light from within fell full upon him, and the astonished laird saw a tiny, well-proportioned man, with delicate features, and golden hair flowing over his shoulders. He wore a cloak of green cloth, lined with daisies. His beautiful face quivered with amusement at the laird's surprise, and he cried triumphantly, "D'ye see me? D'ye see me now, Brockburn?"

"Aye, aye," said the laird, "and seeing's believing."

"Then round with ye!" shouted the man of peace, and once more seizing the laird by the arm, he turned him swiftly round – this time, to the right – and at the third turn the light vanished, and Brockburn and the man of peace were once more alone together in the mist.

"Aweel, Brockburn," said the man of peace, "I'll allow ye're honest, and have a convincible mind. I'm not ill disposed towards ye, and ye shall get safe home, man."

As he spoke he stooped down, and picking up half-a-dozen big stones from the mountainside, he gave them to the laird, saying, "If your good wife asks ye about the stones, say ye got them as a compliment."

Brockburn put them into his pocket, briefly

saying, "I'm obliged to ye," but as he followed the man of peace down the hillside, he found the obligation so heavy, that from time to time he threw a stone away, unobserved, as he hoped, by his companion. When the first stone fell, the man of peace looked sharply round, saying, "What's that?"

"It'll be my feet striking upon the ground," said the laird.

"You're mad," said the man of peace, and Brockburn felt sure that he knew the truth, and was displeased. But as they went on, the stones were so heavy, and bumped his side so hard, that he threw away a second, dropping it as gently as he could. But the sound of its fall did not escape the ears of the man of peace, who cried as before, "What's that?"

"It's just a nasty cough that I have," said the laird.

"Man, you're daft," said the dwarf, with contempt, "that's what ails ye."

The laird now resolved to be prudent, but the heaviness of his burden was so great that after a while he resolved to risk the displeasure of the man of peace once more, and gently slipped a third stone to the ground.

'Third time's lucky,' he thought. But the proverb

failed him, for the dwarf turned as before, shouting, "What's that?"

"It'll be my new shoes that ye hear stumbling upon the big stones," said the laird.

"Ye're drunk, Brockburn, I tell ye so. Ye're drunk!" growled the man of peace, angrily, and the laird dared not drop any more of the gifts. After a while his companion's good humour seemed to return, and he became talkative and generous.

"Ye shall not have to say that ye've been with the Daoiné Shi and are not the better for it," he said. "I'm thinking I'll grant ye three wishes. But choose wisely, man, and don't throw them away."

The laird at once began to cast about in his mind for three wishes sufficiently comprehensive to secure his lifelong prosperity, but the more he beat his brains the less could he satisfy himself.

How many miles he wandered thus, the dwarf keeping silently beside him, he never knew, before he sank exhausted on the ground, saying, "I'm thinking, man, that if ye could bring home to me, in place of bringing me home, I'd doubt your powers no more. It's a far cry to Loch Awe, ye know, and it's a weary long road to Brockburn."

"Is this your wish?" asked the man of peace.

"This is my wish," said the laird.

The words had just scarcely fell from his lips when the whole homestead of Brockburn, the house and all the farm buildings, was planted upon the bleak hillside.

The astonished laird now began to bewail the rash wish which had removed his home from the sheltered and fertile valley where it originally stood to the barren side of a bleak mountain.

The man of peace, however, would not take any hints as to undoing his work of his own accord. All he said was, "If ye wish it away, so it'll be. But then ye'll only have one wish left."

"To leave the steading in such a spot is no to be thought on," sighed the laird, as he spent his second wish in undoing his first. But he cannily added the provision, "And ye may take me with it."

The words were no sooner spoken than the homestead was back in its place, and Brockburn himself was lying in his own bed, with Jock, his favourite collie, barking and licking his face for joy.

"Whisht, whisht, Jock!" said the laird, angrily. "Ye would not bark when I begged, so ye may hand your peace now."

And pushing the collie from him, he sat up in bed and looked anxiously but vainly round the chamber for the man of peace.

"Lie down, lie down," cried his good wife from beside him. "Ye're surely out of your wits. Would ye go wandering about the country again tonight?"

"Where is he?" cried the laird.

"There's not a soul here but your lawful wife and your own dear doggie. Was there anybody that ye expected?" asked his wife.

"The man o' peace, woman!" cried Brockburn.

The Laird and the Man of Peace

"I've one of my wishes to get yet, and I must have it."

"The man's mad!" was his good wife's comment. "Ye've surely forgotten yourself. Ye never believed in the Daoiné Shi before."

"Seeing's believing," said the laird. "I forgathered with a man of peace tonight on the hill, and I wish I just saw him again."

As the laird spoke the window of the chamber was lit up from without, and the man of peace appeared sitting on the window ledge in his daisy-lined cloak, his feet hanging down into the room, the silver shoes glittering as they dangled.

"I'm here, Brockburn!" he cried. "But eh, man! Ye've had your last wish."

And even as the stupefied laird gazed, the light slowly died away, and the man of peace vanished with it.

On the following morning the laird was roused from sleep by loud cries of surprise and admiration.

His wife had been stirring for some hours, and in

emptying the pockets of her good man's coat she had found huge cairngorms of exquisite tint and lustre. Brockburn thus discovered the value of the gifts he had thrown away.

But no subsequent visits to the hillside led to their recovery. Many a time did the laird bring home a heavy pocketful of stones, at his thrifty wife's bidding, but they only proved to be the common stones of the mountainside. The tower could never be distinguished from any other crag, and the Daoiné Shi were visible no more.

Yet it is said that the Laird of Brockburn prospered and throve thereafter, in acre, stall, and steading, as those seldom prosper who have not the good word of the people of peace.

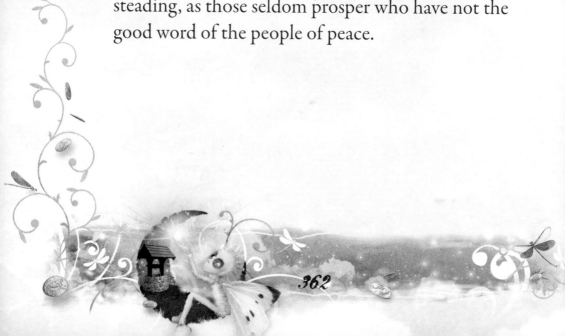

The Laird and the Man of Peace

Peter's Two Wishes

From *Peter Pan in Kensington Gardens*
by J M Barrie

*Peter Pan is a human boy who was left behind in a famous London park
called Kensington Gardens by mistake. He has lived there ever since, a
friend of the fairies. During the day, the fairies hide away from humans,
but they come out to play at night time when the park is locked up.*

*I*t is frightfully difficult to know much at all
about the fairies – indeed, almost the only thing
we know for certain is that there are fairies wherever
there are children. Long ago children were

forbidden in the Gardens, and at that time there
was not a fairy in the place. Then the children were
admitted, and the fairies came trooping in that very
evening. They can't resist following the children,
but you seldom see them, partly because they live in
the daytime behind the railings – where you are not
allowed to go – and also partly because they are so
very cunning.

You remember a good deal about fairies in your
babyhood, which it is a great pity you can't write
down, for gradually you forget, and I have heard of
children who declared that they had never once
seen a fairy. Very likely if they said this in the
Kensington Gardens, they were standing looking at
a fairy all the time. The reason they were cheated
was that she pretended to be something else. This is
one of their best tricks. They usually pretend to be
flowers, because the court sits in the Fairies' Basin,
and there are so many flowers there, and all along
the Baby Walk, that a flower is the thing least likely

I WISH, I WISH

to attract attention. They dress exactly like flowers, and change with the seasons, putting on white when lilies are in and blue for bluebells, and so on.

They like crocus and hyacinth time best of all, as they are partial to a bit of colour, but tulips (except white ones, which are the fairy cradles) they consider garish, and they sometimes put off dressing like tulips for days, so that the beginning of the tulip weeks is almost the best time to catch them.

Peter's Two Wishes

When they think you are not looking they skip along pretty lively, but if you look, and there is no time to hide, they stand quite still pretending to be flowers. Then, after you have passed without knowing that they were fairies, they rush home and tell their mothers they have had such an adventure.

I WISH, I WISH

Numbers of them can also be found along the Baby Walk, which is a famous gentle place (as spots frequented by fairies are called). Once, twenty-four of them had an extraordinary adventure. They were a girls' school out for a walk with the governess, and all wearing hyacinth gowns, when she suddenly put her finger to her mouth, and then they all stood still on an empty bed and pretended to be hyacinths. Unfortunately what the governess had heard was two gardeners coming to plant flowers in that very bed. They were wheeling a handcart with flowers in it, and were surprised to find the bed occupied.

"It's a pity to lift them hyacinths," said the younger of the two men.

"Duke's orders," replied the other, and, having emptied the cart, they dug up the boarding school and put the poor, terrified things in it in five rows. Of course, neither the governess nor the girls dared let on that they were fairies, so they were carted far away to a potting shed, out of which they escaped in the night without their shoes, but there was a great row about it among the parents, and the school's reputation was ruined.

As for their houses, it is no use looking for them, because they are the exact opposite of our houses. You can see our houses by day but you can't see them by dark. Well, you can see their houses by dark, but you can't see them by day, for they are the colour of night, and I never heard of any one yet who could see night in the daytime. This does not mean that they are black, for night has its colours just as day has, but ever so much brighter.

Their blues and reds and greens are like ours with light behind them. Their palace is entirely built of many-coloured glasses, and is the loveliest of all royal residences, but the queen sometimes complains because the common people will peep in to see what she is doing. They are very inquisitive folk, and press quite hard against the glass, and that is why their noses are mostly snubby.

I WISH, I WISH

One of the great differences between the fairies and us is that they never do anything useful. When the first baby laughed for the first time, his laugh broke into a million pieces, and they all went skipping about. That was the beginning of fairies. They look tremendously busy, as if they had not a moment to spare, but if you were to ask them what they are doing, they could not tell you in the least. They are frightfully ignorant, and everything they do is make-believe. It is a very noticeable thing that, in fairy families, the youngest is always chief person, and usually becomes a prince or princess.

The fairies are exquisite dancers, and hold their great balls in the open air, in what is called a fairy ring. For weeks afterwards you can see the ring on the grass. It is not there when they begin, but they make it by waltzing round and round. Sometimes you will find mushrooms inside the ring, and these are fairy chairs that the servants have forgotten to clear away. The chairs and the rings are the only

signs these little people ever leave behind, and they
would remove even these were they not so fond of
dancing that they continue to make merry till the
very moment of the opening of the park gates.

If on such a night we could remain behind in the
gardens, we might see delicious sights. One of the
grandest is when hundreds of fairies hasten to the
ball, the married ones wearing their wedding rings
round their waists, the gentlemen, all in uniform,
holding up the ladies' trains, and linkmen running
in front carrying winter cherries, which are the fairy
lanterns. The supper table, with Queen Mab at the
head, glows with the light of one hundred fireflies,
and behind the queen's chair stands the Lord
Chamberlain, who carries a dandelion on which he
blows when her majesty wants to know the time.

The tablecloth varies according to the seasons,
and in May it is made of chestnut blossom. The way
the fairy servants make them is this: Scores of the
men climb up the trees and shake the branches, and

the blossom falls like snow. Then the lady servants sweep it together by whisking their skirts until it is exactly like a tablecloth, and that is how they get their tablecloth.

Peter Pan is the fairies' orchestra. He sits in the middle of the ring, and they would never dream of having a smart dance nowadays without him. They are grateful little people, too, and at the coming-of-age ball of the princess (they come of age on their second birthday and have a birthday every month) they agreed to grant him the wish of his heart.

The queen ordered him to kneel, and then said that for playing so beautifully she would give him the wish of his heart. Then all the fairies gathered round Peter in order to hear what the wish of his heart was, but for a long time he hesitated, for he was not quite certain what it was himself.

"If I chose to go back to mother," he asked at last, "could you give me that wish?"

Now this question vexed them, for were he to

Peter's Two Wishes

return to his mother they should no longer have his music, so the queen tilted her nose and said, "Pooh, you should ask for a much bigger wish than that."

"Is that quite a little wish?" he inquired.

"As little as this," the queen answered, putting her hands near each other.

"What size is a big wish?" he asked.

She measured it off on her skirt and it was a very handsome length.

Then Peter thought, and said, "Well, I think I shall have two little wishes instead of one big one."

Of course, the fairies felt they could not say no to his request, though his cleverness in asking rather shocked them. He told them that his first wish was to go back to his dear mother, but with the right to return to his home and friends in Kensington Gardens if he found her to be disappointing. His second wish he decided he would hold in reserve until he thought of something that was really worth wishing for.

They tried to dissuade him, and even put obstacles in the way. "I can give you the power to fly to her house," the queen said, "but I can't open the door for you."

"The window I flew out at will be open," Peter said confidently. "Mother always keeps it open in the hope that I may fly back."

"How do you know?" they asked, quite surprised, and, really, Peter could not explain how he knew.

"I just know," he said.

So as he persisted in his wish, they had to grant it. The way they gave him power to fly was this: They all tickled him on the shoulder, and soon he felt a funny itching in that part, and then up he rose higher and higher, and flew away out of the Gardens and over the housetops.

It was so delicious that instead of flying straight to his own home he skimmed away over St Paul's to the Crystal Palace and back by the river and

Peter's Two Wishes

Regent's Park, and by the time he reached his mother's window he had quite made up his mind that his second wish should be to become a bird.

The window was wide open, just as he knew it would be, and in he fluttered, and there was his mother lying asleep. Peter alighted softly on the wooden rail at the foot of the bed and had a good look at her. She lay with her head on her hand, and the hollow in the pillow was like a nest lined with her brown wavy hair. He remembered, though he had long forgotten it, that she always gave her hair a holiday at night. How sweet the frills of her nightgown were! He was very glad she was such a pretty mother.

But she looked sad, and he knew why she looked sad. One of her arms moved as if it wanted to go round something, and he knew what it wanted to go round.

"Oh, mother," said Peter to himself, "if you just knew who is sitting on the rail at the foot of the bed at this very moment."

Very gently he patted the little mound that her feet made, and he could see by her face that she liked it. He knew he had but to say 'Mother' ever so softly, and she would wake up. They always wake up at once if it is you that says their name. Then she

Peter's Two Wishes

would give such a joyous cry and squeeze him tight. How nice that would be to him, and how exquisitely delicious it would be to her. That, I am afraid, is how Peter regarded it. In returning to his mother he never doubted that he was giving her the greatest treat a woman can have. Nothing can be more splendid, he thought, than to have a little boy of your own. How proud of him they are! And very right and proper, too.

But why does Peter sit so long on the rail, and why does he not tell his mother that he has come back to her?

I quite shrink from the truth, which is that he sat there in two minds. Sometimes he looked longingly at his mother, and sometimes he looked longingly at the window. Certainly it would be pleasant to be her boy again, but on the other hand, what times those had been in the Gardens! Was he so sure that he should enjoy wearing clothes again? He popped off the bed and opened some drawers to have a look

377

at his old garments. They were still there, but he could not remember how you put them on. The socks, for instance, were they worn on the hands or on the feet? He was about to try one of them on his hand, when he had a great adventure. Perhaps the drawer had creaked – at any rate, his mother woke up, for he heard her say 'Peter,' as if it was the most lovely word in the language. He remained sitting on the floor and held his breath, wondering how she knew that he had come back. If she said 'Peter' again, he meant to cry 'Mother' and run to her. But she spoke no more, she made little moans only, and when he next peeped at her she was once more asleep, with tears on her face.

It made Peter very miserable, and what do you think was the first thing he did? Sitting on the windowsill, he played a beautiful lullaby to his mother on his pipe. He had made it up himself out of the way she said 'Peter,' and he never stopped playing until she looked happy.

Peter's Two Wishes

He thought this so clever of him that he could scarcely resist wakening his mother to hear her say, 'Oh, Peter, how exquisitely you play.' However, as she now seemed comfortable, he again cast looks at the window.

You must not think that he meditated flying away and never coming back. He had quite decided to be his mother's boy once more, but hesitated about beginning tonight. It was the second wish which troubled him. He no longer intended to make it a wish to be a bird, but not to ask for a second wish seemed wasteful, and, of course, he could not ask for it without returning to the fairies. Also, if he put off asking for his wish too long it might go bad.

And in the end, you know, he flew away. Twice he came back from the window, wanting to kiss his mother, but he feared the delight of it might waken her, so at last he played her a lovely kiss on his pipe, and then he flew back to the gardens.

Peter's Two Wishes

Many nights and even months passed before he asked the fairies to grant his second wish, and I am not sure that I quite know why it was that he delayed so long. One reason was that he had so many goodbyes to say, not only to his particular friends, but to a hundred favourite spots. Then he had his last sail, and his very last sail, and his last sail of all, and so on.

But, mind you, though Peter was so slow in going back to his mother, he was quite decided to go back. The best proof of this was his caution with the fairies. They were most anxious that he should remain in the gardens to play to them, and to bring this to pass they tried to trick him into making such a remark as 'I wish the grass was not so wet,' and some of them danced out of time in the hope that he might cry, 'I do wish you would keep time!' Then they would have said that this was his second wish. But though on occasions he began, "I wish," he always checked himself in time.

So when at last he said to them bravely, "I wish now to go back to mother for ever and always," they had to tickle his shoulders and let him go.

He went in a hurry in the end because he had dreamt that his mother was crying, and he knew the great thing she cried for, and that a hug from her splendid Peter would be the only thing to quickly make her to smile. Oh, he felt sure of it, and so eager was he to be nestling in her arms that this time he flew straight to the window, which was always to be left open for him.

But when at last he reached the window he found that it was closed, and there were strong iron bars upon it. And when he peered inside he saw his mother sleeping peacefully with her arm round another little boy.

Peter called, "Mother! Mother!" but she heard him not. In vain he beat his little limbs against the iron bars. He had to fly back, sobbing, to the Gardens, and he never saw his dear mother again.

Peter's Two Wishes

What a glorious boy he had meant to be to her. Ah, Peter, we who have made the great mistake, how differently we should all act at the second chance. But there is no second chance, not for most of us. When we reach the window it is Lock-out Time. The iron bars are up for life.

The End